ELSE'S JOURNEY

ELSE'S JOURNEY

A STORY OF RESILIENCE

ELIZABETH RITT with KELLEY HARTMAN

Printed in the United States of America

First Printing, 2024

ISBN 978-1-955791-93-9

Library of Congress Control Number: 2024903178

Ordering Information: Special discounts are available on quantity purchases by bookstores, corporations, associations, and others. For details, contact the publisher at sales@braughlerbooks.com or at 937-58-BOOKS.

For questions or comments about this book, please write to info@braughlerbooks.com.

Else's Journey: A Story of Resilience

Allowing for the intelligence of an adult memory seventy years later, this is a work of historical fiction, except for some names and identifying details that have been changed to respect individuals' privacy.

Elizabeth Ritt with Kelley Hartman

Dedication

This book is dedicated to Else who inspired us with her story as a young woman surviving WWII.

Prologue

November 2023

Dear Mom,

Growing up in a working-class community in Chicago during the 1960s, I had no idea of the experiences you endured during adolescence and into young adulthood. However, I knew there was something special about the way you loved me unconditionally, modeled empathy through acts of kindness, and ensured I felt safe and well-nourished.

As a child, I knew you were different because of your European accent. I remember countless family gatherings where home-cooked meals and desserts were central to our time together. These gatherings were often held on Sundays when everyone took time away from work and home duties to enjoy each other's company. You were the more serious one out of the family making sure we minded our manners but still managed to have fun.

While you would share bits and pieces of your life, coupled with amusing stories, it was not until April 2020 that I uncovered the real story of what made you so different. We could not see each other in person due to the pandemic so our regular check-in calls became our way to stay in touch. At first, we chatted about the weather, the latest news, family activities, friends, and changes at the senior living facility where you resided. However, as the "lockdown" continued, I sensed that you were increasingly sad and lonely due to the protracted social isolation. We were separated in the physical sense, and I yearned to hug you, listen to music, and share meals.

You were my mother, best friend, and an exceptionally good listener. It was incredible how you managed to sit for hours and engage in stories about my children, work, and hopes for the future. You had a way of making me feel like I was the most important person in the world.

One day, I remember calling you a bit early for our chat and could hear country music in the background. Suddenly, it dawned on me that I did not know why you listened to this genre of music. So, I asked about it because it was such a divergence from classical music, which you listened to in your early years.

You responded, "That is an easy question. It is because I love the stories told in country music, and it was a clever way to learn English." We laughed but that day started our journey of loving and respectful conversations about your life as a child and young woman growing up in Yugoslavia. I realized that there was so much I did not know about you and at times felt guilty that I was not more inquisitive.

I could hardly wait for our next conversation about your life. Often, you left me hanging in anticipation of the next story, surprise, or character-building experience. Not sure if it was intentional but it certainly kept me calling you. Now it was my turn to listen intently to stories and it became clear that you had many to tell.

Whenever we spoke we would just pick up our conversation as if there was no lapse in time at all. As we talked for hours over the phone, your brilliant memories emerged with incredible beauty and unwavering clarity. Your ability to share experiences from over seventy years ago as if they happened yesterday kept me in suspense and wanting more.

I lost you in the physical sense on December 25, 2020, at the age of ninety-four, seventy of which you lived in Chicago. Your soft voice, loving smile, and magnificent ability to tell stories will live on in all those you met along the way. You dreamt of being a teacher, but I know your life took a radically different path. However, you were indeed a fine teacher and taught me how to live.

Love always,
Elizabeth

Else: Betschkerck, 1939

The morning is whipped air with sunshine you can nearly taste. My eyes are still closed when I hear them shouting, shrieking as they run toward the house. I recognize their voices immediately: Anica, with her round cheeks and springy gait; Sera, her dark hair, plaited down her back, and her smile, wide and toothy. Their laughter tells me this won't be a day for chores or helping Father stock the shelves at the store. This is a day for breathing in the summer air and running to Lake Bega, three friends linking arms, our pockets stuffed with jam-filled krapfen.

The heat of summer simmers with anticipation. We're thirteen, preoccupied with nylons and ribbons, but also with the tenderness of anguish as we try to stretch ourselves from childhood into a world filled with adult things, like the sweetness of young romance and a desire for freedom.

"What do you think of Zivko?" Anica asks, the two of us floating on our backs in the lake, our hair dipping below the surface of the water.

"The one with the mole above his eyebrow?" Sera responds, as she wades in, adding, "The boy with the mole that sprouts hair!?" before

doubling over in laughter.

Anica springs upright, flicking water in Sera's direction. "Well, what about David? You write his name all over your slate during spelling and it looks like he never washes his hair."

Smiling, my arms float up. I slowly push them down to my side, letting the water roll over my stomach as my body moves with the current. The water covers my ears, muffling Anica and Sera's shrieks as they splash water on each other. I close my eyes and feel the sun warm my face, content to stay away from the teasing. Both David and Zivko are childish, and peculiar. Instead, I think of the boy who picks me wildflowers on his walk home from school.

I feel a splash of water hit my face, followed by a playful shout. My eyes shoot open.

"Sera!"

I swing my feet through the water and try to press myself upright against the river's sandy bottom. My toes hit the silt as the ground shifts, crumbling beneath my feet. The water wraps around my body, squeezing me like a sieve as the strength of the undercurrent pulls fast, then faster into the cool depths of the lake. I open my mouth to shout for help. Water flows into my throat, choking the words until the only thing that sputters out is a gasp that wheezes against the humidity pressing against my forehead. My lungs expand with the water, swallowing river and dirt and algae, the current whipping into my nose, stinging my eyes.

My arms struggle to fight and thrash against the undertow but the water presses them to my side. The heaviness of the river groans against my lungs, my legs, my stomach, and my mind until it goes blank, then yellow, then black.

Chapter 1

My earliest memories from my birthplace, Tschetereg, Yugoslavia, were the smell of the spruce pine trees in the snap of fall and the bells ringing from Saint John of Nepomuk Catholic Church as they began their toll for afternoon mass or evening vigil.

I remember the table where I'd sit quietly, tracing letters on scrap paper next to my older brother, Henry, as my younger sister, Mary, played with her dolls and my youngest brother, Joshi, grabbed at the hem of my mother's skirt. My mother, Lissie, was a beautiful woman, sturdy and short in stature with light brown hair, her smile soft and confident, reflecting her strength and countenance as the backbone of our family. My father, Jens, was also a man of conviction—a visionary whose dreams were woven with a kind of gentle optimism that filled our home with sweetness.

Mother would say that she didn't think she'd love Father, a man she barely knew when their families arranged their marriage. Lissie was just shy of her seventeenth birthday when she exchanged vows with Jens, newly twenty years old. She didn't want to be married, least of all to a stranger, and resented him for being the man she was betrothed to, even though they'd only spoken a few words. The bitterness didn't dissipate with the marriage ceremony, nor with the weeks and months that followed, but she would remember, on especially fragrant spring days, the way Father's eyes warmed when she met him at the altar; how he didn't look away but held her gaze during the entire course of the marriage rites.

"Perhaps his heart is good," she let herself wonder as they sat, strangers, side-by-side at their marriage feast, their families toasting their prosperity and future progeny.

By the end of their first year of marriage, Lissie and Jens were still more strangers than spouses, but she learned that he did indeed have a good heart. He would bring her soft blooms from the meadow outside their small home and touch the small of her back when she walked through the threshold of a room ahead of him. She, in turn, learned that he loved goulash on cold winter days and room temperature beer on long summer nights; that he relished bringing the best bits of that day's bake home for her; that love, for Jens, was like a warm breeze on a still, spring morning, soft and gentle. And she, too, learned to love him.

Tschetereg was small, only five hundred or so people, but the land filled in the gaps with lush deciduous trees that would burst into color as the summer sun cooled into kaleidoscopic autumn, wind whipping colors off the oaks that stood in contrast to the evergreen spruce peppered amongst their colorful, yet temporal counterparts. And because of this, or perhaps in spite of it, the smell of decaying leaves that permeated every autumn since those early years in Tschetereg was masked by the delicious spice of needles.

We spoke Serbian at home, but by the time I was five, I had been sent to the school attached to the Catholic church to learn German. The rough, guttural sounds scratched my throat as I barked out numbers and colors and told my classmate that I liked her bows at the ends of her neat braids, and everything else a precocious five-year-old might have said.

In German, we learned arithmetic and history, national unity, and how to spell words in our new language. And also about John of Nepomuk, the Bohemian saint and namesake of our church, who was drowned in the Vltava River in 1393, and who ultimately became an exalted protector against floods and drownings. I remember thinking of the Bega River that wound its way through green marshland on the outskirts of town, and wondered how something so peaceful and serene could be so deadly.

In 1935, when I was eight and my memory began to come into focus, we left Tschetereg. The town was small, perhaps too small for the dreams of my father, but it held everything and everyone we knew—my mother's parents, her sisters and brother, our house with the restaurant and the ballroom. The center of the world was Tschetereg until my father sold everything, then suddenly, it wasn't.

Betschkerck was only 20 kilometers southwest of Tschetereg, but much larger with 45,000 people and imposing stone architecture, like Bukovac's Palace with its balconies and rounded arches. In the center of town, Freedom Square was surrounded by the rows of windows and columns that typified the buildings that made up the city, most painted in yellows and blues and peaches—colors that felt so different from the lush greens and chestnut browns woven into the landscape of our old home.

The year we moved, Betschkerck was renamed Petrovgrad. By the time we left Betschkerck, it had been renamed again to

Zrenjanin. Later the city would have four names, depending on what you spoke: Großbetschkerek in German, Nagybecskerek in Hungarian, Zreňanin in Slovak, and Зрењанин in Serbian. Eventually, I became fluent in each language, but once I left, I never returned to call the city by any of its names.

Chapter 2

In 1935, Betschkerck, then Petrovgrad, was teeming with people who built churches, attended synagogues, and filled hospitals, and was complete with a large train station that connected us to cities even bigger, in Yugoslavia, in Hungary—in far-off places like Munich or Vienna.

We had moved so my father could take specialized courses in business management and entrepreneurship. My father opened a bakery that was connected to a grocery store. Like in Tschetereg, we lived onsite, in a house that was connected to the businesses. This time it was bigger, though not only to accommodate his enterprising spirit. Our family had grown with the addition of another little brother, Frankie, and a new dog named Shipsi.

The memories of our new home became more pronounced as I grew from a child into young adulthood. Lessons at the public elementary school near the center of town; the smell of bread baking as my father scored pale, unbaked loaves, readying them for the oven; the backroom of the grocery store with its earthy smell of dried beans and the pickled fragrance of sliced cabbage and sausage, carefully preserved in salt and vinegar; the stench of manure from the pig sty next to the vegetable garden, which sat next to the house and ran a full city block.

Most of the neighbors' houses were still lit by gas or lantern, but ours was heated with coal and wood and had electricity. It was a luxury out of necessity for my father's ambition. To operate the store and bakery, we needed artificial light, bright and blue.

We measured our days in loaves of bread and pairs of black patent leather shoes. In the mornings I'd dress in a smart black dress with a white collar—a uniform I wore alongside the forty-five other girls at school. The shoes, shiny as they were, would scuff easily as we walked through town.

School occupied my time until the early afternoon. Once we were dismissed, I'd head home to help my father with the store, but not before I slowed my gait to walk with my best friends, Anica and Sera, through the center of town to look at the window displays: the music shop filled with newly delivered accordions trimmed in red; the jewelry store, with delicate gold necklaces on display.

There was always a symphony of language—Serbian melting into Hungarian into Slovak into German. While I could fit myself within the tapestry of conversation easily, our family didn't fit neatly into the classifications that surrounded us. It was generational: my mother's parents, immigrants from Alsace Lorraine, moved from one part of Europe that made shifting borders and changing nationalities the heartbeat of their culture (platters of German-made sauerkraut and sausage ordered in French), to another, rich with amalgamation. My father was German, which meant we were German and French, but here that simply translated into Yugoslavian. In Betschkerck, it was easy for my family to reside somewhere in the middle. Father baked heavy loaves of bread for the Hungarians, and corn bread for the Serbian workers at the brick factory, our lives a constant swirl of culture that seemed to blend into one.

Father had imparted the value of hard work early, giving all of us, including Frankie, little tasks around the store or bakery when we were old enough to hold things steadily in our hands. There was something delightful about feeling important in some small way as we picked up dried beans that had fallen on the floor, carried loaves from the ovens to the baskets where customers would select that day's bread, and eventually, worked the till, carefully counting out change.

But, I was too curious to be content with our simple chores at home. As we left school, my brain would swirl with everything we had learned. There was too much to see, too much to know—even the brilliant colors of our town square reflected a kaleidoscopic pattern of culture that I so desperately wanted to understand. I could never imagine leaving home, but the thrill of learning expanded my small world in ways that were intoxicating.

"No, I mean, what do you *really* want to do," Sera pressed me one day as we walked.

Like Anica, she was tall with dark hair. All three of us wore our hair in soft curls, delicately pinned back to reflect the style we all desperately tried to follow. We had become fast friends at school, the three of us striking that precarious balance of studious and social, absorbing everything from arithmetic to buzzy gossip like the adolescent sponges that we were.

"I told you! I want to be a teacher." I shifted my books from one arm to another.

It was the first warm day of spring and as we left the schoolhouse, it was as if the flowers had started to bud while we sat inside working on our spelling lessons. Anica ran ahead to pick a crocus.

"I want to be a teacher too, Sera!" she yelled back at us as she plucked a blooming lavender-colored bud from the grass. "What's wrong with that?"

"Nothing, I guess, but what if you could do *anything*?" Sera did a cartwheel "I'd be an actress!" I laughed as Anica applauded Sera's acrobatics.

When I got home, I changed from my school uniform into work clothes, including a canvas apron that I'd wear in the store. I thought about Sera's question again: What would I do if I really could do anything—anything at all? I looked out the window, saw the meadow's first buds cresting over its verdant green and smiled.

"I'd be a teacher," I said softly, to no one but myself. What a way, I thought, to learn more about the world while staying here in this beautiful place.

◆◆◆◆

In the summer, we'd run to Bega Lake, a beautiful pool of deep blue water. It was on the outskirts of town, but near enough to our house that we could slip away each weekend for a few hours, wading into the cool waters as the afternoon heat set in. Henry and I would rush ahead while Mary and Joshi ran after us, trying to catch up.

Henry, as the oldest, was naturally our leader. He was stoic but affable as we readied ourselves for school, helping move us along so we wouldn't be late. But when we'd head to the lake, he'd shed his protective, almost paternal, sensibilities and create games for us to play while we waded in the water and splashed around.

Mary loved our water games. She seemed to love everything, and everyone. Her spirit was like a balloon, always cheerfully floating up, up, up, ready to embrace even the smallest joy as if it were the rich, most delicious, cream of life. And if Mary was the spark that made every adventure more exciting, Joshi kept us on our toes. Always getting into mischief, he was the first person I looked for if I noticed a chicken wandering outside our yard, far from its coop. Or, if I felt a splash of water as I sat on the soft silt beach of the lake, soaking the hem of my skirt.

On days when the sun felt extra warm, the dew on the grass sparkling just ever so slightly against the blue sky of a perfect day, I'd put little Frankie on my hip and let him join us, shrieking as we splashed water onto his chubby legs.

But this was the truth that we were too naive to understand: that the water was beautiful until it wasn't. I only knew to trust its blueness, to absorb the sweet serenity of the wind tickling the shore as I waded into the lake. In Betschkerck, in school, Anica, Sera, and I had learned that water was clear and colorless, shapeless and still, but on a warm summer morning, as I floated on my back in the coolness of the lake, I discovered the water of John of Nepomuk, relentless and wrathful, as it began to push my body down, into the darkness. Altogether unforgiving.

As the blackness threatened to overtake, water pressing on my lungs until they burst, I grasped for the saint of my childhood. Where was he, this saint of drowning? In the black, I saw my father baking bread, Frankie running after Mary, my mother in her starched apron, her neck framed by her favorite collar with the scalloped edges. Shipsi licked my face as I laughed, or perhaps cried, gasping in the darkness.

The wetness from the dog's tongue melted against my face, my stomach lurching with the realization that there was no dog, only river water that I retched up on the soft bank of the lake. A white light washed everything into purple, then into the blue sky I was staring at as I lay on my back, my shoulders shaking.

Anica and Sera later told me that Henry appeared as I disappeared beneath the water. That he was able to wade into the lake and pull me from the undertow, heavy and limp, before I coughed up all the water that had flooded my body. But I could only remember the suffocating darkness and the lake that tried to swallow me whole.

Chapter 3

In 1940, the Nazis came. I sometimes try to remember if the weight of their occupation hung heavy within hours of their arrival, but the truth was that the reality of their presence crept in slowly. The angled curves of Serbian Cyrillic were replaced with the sloping calligraphy of German, first in the market, then the churches, then finally, the schools.

There was a flattening—of life, of the multifaceted brilliance I had grown to love. The Germans seized our town but it felt more like a strangulation, suffocating the life out of our country, out of our Betschkerck. A heaviness lingered as we walked to town, inquired after neighbors, and did our lessons. The persistent nervousness was a constant companion, one that gave way to dull anxiety that never seemed to leave. Everything in our life was poised toward survival, toward staying in Yugoslavia.

My parents had bought a country cottage for our family months before the first Nazi insignia flew on our town halls. It was a small, bucolic place with its own parcel of land. It was decided that we'd move once the grocery store and bakery were more established and we didn't need to be so close. Quaint, with three rooms, it was a declaration of the future, one with pretty lace curtains and a large wooden table like the one we had at the house attached to the store.

While we waited for the day to come when we'd move from the city and the store to the sweet, serenity of wide, expansive spaces, we'd crowd into the kitchen—sometimes as many as ten of us, including the two bakers who worked with my father, and my grandmother. Oma, my father's mother, lived with us and kept her quiet spirit on the periphery of our busy family life. I loved her dearly. There was something about her presence that smoothed the edges of my teenage anxiety and the uneasiness of the occupation. When I returned home from school, she'd be sitting in the kitchen, her dress, usually black, draped over its seat and obscuring her legs, which were thin with age. Oma would position herself near the window so she could look over the fields and watch us walk toward the house.

"Ah, Else. And how was your day?" she'd murmur as I stepped across the threshold, never turning to face me, but always seeming to anticipate my presence. I'd hang up my coat and walk to Oma's chair. Occasionally she'd be darning one of father's socks or peeling a small bag of potatoes for mother.

"Hello, Oma," I'd say, kissing her cheek, soft with wrinkles, before I'd try to remember something sweet to share with her.

Some days it was a simple observation: "The tulips around the square have started to bloom, Oma. Pinks and yellows and purples! It's such a beautiful sight."

Other days it was the seed of a dream: "I was thinking on my walk home, how wonderful it would be to become a teacher."

Her response was always the same: "Of course, sweet Else," as she squeezed my hand or held my face. I'd close my eyes, imagining the same scene in the sweetness of the country cottage. I'd bring her flowers too, I decided, from the garden I'd surely have. There would be irises and mountain buttercups, with overflowing mounds of lily-of-the-valley.

In the months before the Nazis arrived, we sat at the table, lapping up bowls of my mother's beef goulash and noodles, sopping up the gravy with fresh bread, unwinding stories. I realize now, embedded in those threads of the things we shared were the whispers of what we wanted, a village of our own kind of quaint cottages, built on the banks of dreams that dotted the Bega River, soon to be destroyed.

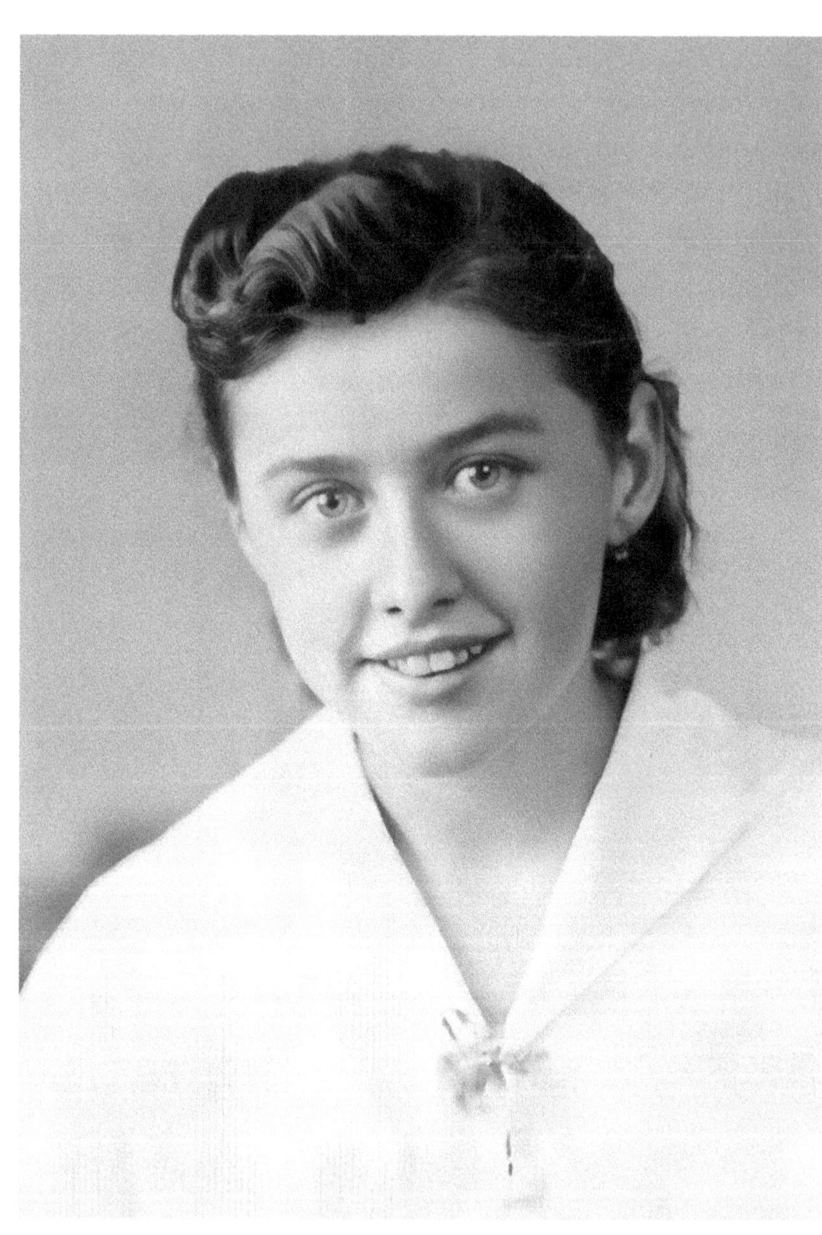

Chapter 4

Slowly everything changed, until who we were and where we were felt unrecognizable. To us, anyway. Not to them. According to the Nazis, we were German. My *Abitur*, my high school diploma, was revised from Serbian to German, stamped with an official Nazi seal. Our community of languages was funneled into German, and only German. I had stopped my regular German lessons once we moved to Betschkerck, and now that I was fourteen, I could barely remember any of the formal grammar. I spoke the language on the street, but in order to live in our new reality, I had to learn how to read, how to write, how to properly use *hoch Deutsch.* No longer merely conversational, my family's survival was predicated by the correctness and formality of language and the way we conducted our lives.

Even with the occupation, my dream of becoming a teacher still seemed practical. With our *Abiturs* in hand, Henry and I went to Werschetz, a town 40 kilometers southeast of Betschkerck, to attend the teachers college. It was a smaller town, but still lively, filled with different languages and people. But when we arrived, the starkness of the crimson flags, their black Swastikas against white circles, spoke of a city far different from where we had come.

"Henry, what do you make of this," I muttered through clenched teeth as we descended from the train and walked across the platform, Nazi insignia everywhere. Henry said nothing, but held my arm close to him as we walked quickly through the town square to the college dorm buildings. He looked forward, his face strict and silent, but I could tell his eyes were scanning the buildings quickly, trying to assess our new surroundings.

Werschetz's occupation looked different from Betschkerck. We had been aware of the Nazis, but only as an oppressive nuisance that kept us on guard. Here, they seemed to be celebrated and I couldn't quite understand it.

Henry pulled me under a small overhang on the edge of the main square.

"Look Else," he began, his voice practically a whisper. "I don't really know what to make of everything. But it seems like Werschetz feels differently about the Nazis than we do, and I think we need to be very careful."

I nodded. I trusted Henry implicitly. He had always held himself well, projecting an image of confidence and physical assuredness, but as he spoke, I felt the certainty of his demeanor waver.

"We're safe, right?" I asked quietly. A flash of fear crossed his face before he straightened his back, smoothed the front of his jacket, and looked across the square at a Nazi flag fluttering in the wind.

"We're safe, Else." He squeezed my arm. "We're safe. We just need to focus on doing what we came here to do, which is to become teachers." He paused, putting his hands on both my shoulders. As though reading my mind, he continued:

"Mother, Father, the boys, Mary—they'll be okay." I nodded. My face suddenly felt hot as my eyes welled.

"Else, look at me." I lifted my head, unable to prevent a tear from slipping down my cheek.

"Else," Henry's face was strict. "Else…." He repeated, his voice wavering for only a moment before regaining its characteristic strength. This unsteadiness, so subtle that anyone other than a sister would have missed it, felt so foreign to my ear. The way Betschkerck had molded itself around our occupiers felt different than it was here. If our hometown had recognized our new reality with a resigned acceptance, Werschetz had openly embraced theirs with a boldness that recalibrated normalcy.

"Mother and Father will make sure everything is okay," he continued, his tone firm. "You've wanted to be a teacher for too long to let the occupation and things we can't control distract you. Besides," he said, then cracked a small smile. "Father knows that everyone needs bread, even German soldiers."

We stayed in dorms, me with four other female roommates in a small, but cozy room, while Henry was across town in the male dorms. I hated being so far from my family. The world was shifting but I still craved the comforts of home, no matter how much they changed with the arrival of our occupiers. After a few weeks, however, I realized how much I also relished the quietude of my studies. Without the distractions of Joshi's impish pranks or keeping careful measure of the store's till, or house chores, I found myself fully immersed in classes, my mind in a state of constant expanse as I read and wrote and debated with other students.

Even as I turned my attention outward, away from Betschkerck and toward the newness of my education, Mary and I wrote to each other incessantly.

Darling sister,

Good news! We were able to secure music lessons in town and I'm finally learning how to play the accordion. When you and Henry come home, we'll be able to play together! And now that I have my own instrument, I won't have to borrow yours. I know, it seems ridiculous to add another accordion to our growing collection, but this way we won't have to take turns. With the violin, the piano, and the accordions, we'll keep everyone entertained!

All my love, Mary

Dearest Mary,

Oh, that's wonderful! You know how much I love my accordion and I know Henry will be excited to hear that you've picked it up as well. I know he misses music. Sometimes I wonder if he should have studied to be a musician, not a teacher, since he's the most talented out of all of us. How are things going with the store? With Mother? Are you managing the purchasing trips well? I hate that we have to travel to the wholesale district to buy anything for the store....these new regulations make it so difficult and I know it causes Father even more stress than normal. He's mentioned how much he hates the ration cards. How are your spirits? Tell me more about your accordion lessons!

Love, Else

Dear Else,

Oh, how much I miss you. And Henry. There's not much to report about the accordion lessons. Air raid sirens have been going off regularly so I've missed most of them or they've ended early...and anyways, it's better to help Father with the store. And Mother prefers that I stay close to home with Joshi and Frankie. I hate the sirens, Else. The first time I heard one, I nearly cried, I was so scared. But now, they've become so frequent that they're just a nuisance. Frankie says he likes them because it means he doesn't have to go to school. I wish I had better news, but

everyday there seems to be something new for concern. I just hope that the air raid sirens stop.
Love, Mary

Else,

I haven't heard from you in a few weeks and assume that school is keeping you very busy but I had to write. Remember the shops that line the main street, downtown? The jewelry store whose window we love to gaze into? And that darling little bakery owned by the Zalabak family? A few days ago, the German government placed big red stamps on the store signs of all the shops owned by our Jewish friends...and stole everything that they had inside. They still open the shops, but now they're nearly empty, each with a big sign that reads, "Jewish Store." Mother is horrified. Father too.
I wish you were here.
Love, Mary

That winter, as the days shortened and frigid air blanketed Werschetz, I used my studies to push the news from home away from the coziness of my teachers college. Most nights my roommates and I would make a pot of tea, wrapping ourselves in quilts as we talked about the day, before returning to our schoolwork. On weekends, we'd walk through town, looking at delicate trinkets in the shop windows and finding little treats to try. Trinkets and treats became more and more rare as the weeks and months of the occupation increased, but still we found delight in our camaraderie.

Six months after our arrival, my mother appeared at my front door. She had taken the two-hour journey from Betschkerck by horse-drawn wagon, but her hat was still perfectly pinned in place. Standing in the doorway of my dorm, she announced that she was there to fetch both my brother and me. The air had begun to tremble with uncertainty, but I could only think of my dream—a singular desire to become a teacher.

"But Henry's here, mother," I protested. "He's making sure we stay safe."

The sternness of her mouth was pronounced, her lips pursed together. Her eyes, soft with empathy, held firm her focus: to be so far away from home was dangerous. The fabric of our world was unraveling, slowly, and keeping the threads of our family tightly wound was her mission, no matter how thankless and impossible.

Together, the three of us left the teachers college and returned to Betschkerck. That night, back in my childhood bed, with Mary sleeping next to me, I tried to be steady. Perhaps I was trying, in my own way, to be brave as well. My heart was broken. To leave such a place, to end my studies early—I hated it. Everything had already changed so much: sirens, speaking only German, curfews. "Why this too?" I whispered to myself as a tear slipped down my cheek. The future, once neatly mapped out, now seemed foggy and indecipherable. I felt my stomach heave, pressure on my chest, and without realizing it, began to cry. Mary reached over, grabbed my hand, and squeezed it tightly.

◆◆◆◆

How to describe the air in Betschkerck once we returned? It felt sour, like rancid butter and burnt, like the loaves the apprentice at my father's bakery would leave in the oven for too long. Mary hadn't lied to me in her letters, but she also hadn't prepared me for how different home would feel.

The morning after we returned, Mary and I went to the center of town to run errands for our mother. The morning mist was still evaporating off the cobblestoned squares, the skies grayed with fog in the brisk chill of a late January day. We needed to find Mother a few extra yards of increasingly scarce fabric for a pair of curtains she was sewing for the back room of the bakery. With each passing day, the desire to enshroud ourselves within the cocoon of home felt more than necessary; our need for privacy was imperative to our sanity. Curtains were closed midday and by evening time, under the flickering glow of the kitchen lightbulb, Father told his stories, his bakers laughing, Mother rolling her eyes or spitting out sharp jabs with her wickedly fast tongue that sent the room laughing. Almost like nothing had changed. But only almost.

That morning, in the cool of the early morning, as our breath moistened the scarves wrapped tightly around our necks, Mary and I shriveled against the harshness, our world newly awash in gray. As I turned the corner, I saw Mr. Zalabak, the baker whose shop sat on the main thoroughfare of town. He wasn't my father's competitor. Our shop and his sold different kinds of goods to different kinds of people, Zalabak's catering mostly to our Jewish friends, but we knew his family from the markets where we'd get bags of salt and flour for that week's run of orders. As we passed his shop in the cool light of winter, blue and silver, I saw his back hunched over to lock his empty bakery, the drips from the red stamp almost frozen against the big shop window that faced the empty early morning street. As he turned to leave, our eyes locked for a moment; my breath caught in my throat. Around his neck was a wooden sign on a frayed rope, the word *Jude* in calligraphy with sharp points that seemed to stab any eye that read it.

His eyes were tired and empty, but filled with a kind of dull pain that seeps into your blood until you forget it's still there, still lingering, still waiting to snap.

"Mary…"

I gasped out my sister's name. She lowered her head sharply, wrapping her arms around my center and with a sharp squeeze, and turned my body toward home. My neck still craned, my eyes searching into the alley where Mr. Zalabak had disappeared into the darkness.

Chapter 5

Mother's cries were soft, pillowy sobs she tried to muffle into her apron. But as I ironed Henry's shirts, I could hear her on the other side of the wall where she and Father were discussing the books and ledgers for the grocery store and bakery.

Henry meandered into the room where, surrounded by piles of freshly laundered shirts and pants, I was attempting to make sense of what the men needed before they left the next day. Pragmatism, I was learning, was one way to survive, or at the very least, to numb the ache.

"I've made up a pile of four shirts for you to pack. Do you think that'll be enough?" I stretched my arms out to Henry, neatly folded squares of white cotton and buttons in my hands.

"Else, thank you," he said quietly, taking the pile. He laughed softly. "I probably won't need this many. If anything, they'll make sure to give us exactly what they want us to wear. What about cigarettes and sugar biscuits? You have any of those in there?"

I slapped his arm, trying not to smile, my mouth curling upwards even as I tried to scold him.

"Henry, stop. I'm trying to be serious."

The truth was, I didn't want to be serious. I wanted to go back to our nights around the dinner table, the raucous laughing when Henry tried to do impressions of customers—especially mean old Mr. Pizer, who always looked like he'd eaten a rotten lemon. I wanted more nightly stories from Father and Albert, the head baker, who lived with us. Now we were readying them to leave.

A week earlier, word had finally spread to our little town: all men, of German ethnicity, between the ages of eighteen and forty-five, were required to join the German army. Days later, Henry and Father received their written orders. Henry, his birthday just months before, was freshly eligible. Father, silver hair at his temples, only barely qualified. There was also the boy from school, the one who brought me bouquets of wildflowers, and made me blush with little treats from the shops in town. The week the orders came, he asked me to meet him in the town square. I saw him stride toward me, papers clutched in hand, his face strict with seriousness.

"Wait for me?" he whispered, as he pulled me in for a hug. Too young to know much beyond the racing of my heart, I nodded my head and tried not to cry.

We didn't know how old Albert was, but he'd started grumbling as soon as the tanks rolled into Freedom Square weeks earlier.

"You know what's next, don't you?" Albert spit out under his breath, shoving trays filled with small mounds of unbaked bread into the racks that he and Father kept next to the oven.

For days he kept unusually silent, coming early and staying late, as if the bakery, with its familiar warmth, would insulate us from what was happening in the town square. Maybe he thought that if he didn't leave, nothing would change: the cup of coffee he and my father shared in the morning; the instinctive way he knew how to pinch the dough into rounds before they went in the oven; how he'd always find flour in his hair when he washed up before dinner; bowls of my mother's goulash after a long day of work.

There was a heaviness that began to creep into the air, moving around us, flattening even the most jovial stories around the dinner table. One morning, as I walked into the kitchen to pour a cup of tea before opening the grocery store, I saw Albert standing in the window, his body unmoving, his hands frozen, a dish towel threaded between his fingers. Slowly I walked behind him, curious to see what held him spellbound in the early morning hours.

The sun was rising over the snow-laden field, transforming the white downs into blues and purples that blossomed against the golden lavender of dawn. It was the landscape of my childhood, so steadfast, and yet, in the blue light of a winter's morning, altogether delicate and fragile. It held an otherworldly beauty I had never noticed until then.

◆◆◆◆

The expectation should have forewarned us; nonetheless, news of the conscription sucked the air out of our bodies. The alternative was punishment by death, and even then, our family's businesses and activities in town made us conspicuous citizens who'd surely bear the brunt of any transgression made by my father and Henry.

The morning they left, the cloudless sky felt relentless. No matter how hard we tried, there was no hiding our fear and anger. Oma sat silently in the front room as we hurried about, gathering last-minute items. I saw a small book of stories on the table, grabbed it, and shoved it into Henry's bag. I couldn't imagine him in basic training, but I could see him sitting by the lake, under a tree, absorbed in his reading, his glasses slowly slipping down his nose.

"For his days off," I told myself as I closed the bag, knowing the book would most likely stay buried.

Mary attempted a smile as she held out a small parcel of food toward Henry, who suddenly looked much older than his newly eighteen years of age. "There should be enough here to get you to the training camp."

Henry pressed his lips together, bobbing his head in thanks as he took it from her hands. I kept my mouth firm, the heat behind my cheeks flushing my face, red almost too eager to betray the tears I was holding back. Joshi and Frankie held back until my father drew them close. "You'll watch out for the girls, right boys?" Joshi nodded solemnly while Frankie, as if embarrassed by the gravitas of Father's command, shuffled his feet and looked over at Mother.

Henry turned to Oma, her face stoic, and leaned down to gently kiss her weathered cheek. Father was next. Her mouth wavered, crumpling into itself as he knelt in front of her, holding her small hands in his.

"Goodbye, Mother," my father whispered, his eyes clear but lacking their normal luster. "I'll be back soon." He kissed her cheek and paused to wrap his arms around her slight frame.

We didn't know that Oma would pass away a few weeks into their service; that mother and Mary and I would drape ourselves in mourning and attempt to navigate a sadness that bloomed into anger, attaching itself to the grief that had come out of the occupation. But maybe Father did as he lingered at the nape of his mother's neck, at once a boy in need of comfort and a man facing unwanted duty.

Mother stood back as we took turns hugging Henry, and we reached up on tippytoes to kiss Father's cheek. Her stance was silent, her apron crisp, as it was every morning. Her eyes followed my father as he embraced Mary; Henry as he tousled Joshi and Frankie's hair, then put his arm around my shoulders, squeezing me into his side.

Father then gently embraced Mother, holding her head against his chest as he closed his eyes. He cupped her face and whispered something in her ear. Her eyes crinkled, as if to smile, then filled with tears, but I don't remember her crying. She held herself strong and tall as she sent her husband and her son to fight in a war we didn't want, for a cause we didn't understand, for a country that wasn't ours.

We lingered in the doorway watching them walk down the path to the road that would lead them to the train station. As we watched them, the minutes grew heavy, stretching into hours until it felt like we had been standing for days, our father and brother walking away from us for what felt like centuries.

It was easy, then, for me to misinterpret mother's silence as strength. But as the years passed and the war crept into every corner of our lives, I learned that silence was survival. Her silence was the only way she could watch them leave. Otherwise, she would have screamed.

Chapter 6

We had a bakery and no bakers, a grocery store and no grocer. Perhaps it was a bit unfair to have painted ourselves as despairing—both my mother and I had run the businesses alongside my father—but he had been the backbone of each operation. Now he and Albert were gone, but the customers expecting bread delivery remained. And it was one of our only tethers (no matter how tenuous) to some kind of financial security.

The German seizure of Betschkerck suffocated our access to goods, which meant that acquiring supplies and ingredients for the grocery store and bakery was no longer as simple as scheduling a delivery with Mr. Petrović from the market. Instead, we were instructed to go to the wholesale district on the other side of town to purchase what we needed, which would then be sold via ration ticket to our customers. Everyone was required to register the size of their families with the local city hall in order to receive a book of tickets that specified the amount of food based on how many people they needed to feed. Our profit margins had already started to suffer with the onset of the war, but with the occupation and the restriction of commodities, the imposed constrictions on daily life made money even tighter.

The morning after the men left, my mother and I stood in the bakery's kitchen. The ovens were already cold. She ran her fingers along the edge of the counter, stopping to brush away a piece of hardened dough that the normally meticulous Albert had missed the day before.

"We can't rely solely on the grocery store to get us through this," she finally said.

Standing in the cold bakery, I told mother I could help with the runs to the market, but we knew that without Father and Henry, our family was even more vulnerable and any risk we took, no matter how small, would put us all in danger. It had become common to see Nazi trucks in front of the homes of our Jewish neighbors, with a parade of chairs and tables and furs from the house into an open truck until every room was bare. Our friends, standing outside as their belongings were stolen from them, were powerless to do anything. We all were powerless. We didn't know that soon after the furniture disappeared, so too would the people. We only knew that our life had stretched out into a thin line on which we could only hope to balance. One misstep and we'd fall into the darkness.

Father, Henry, and Albert had been forced to join the army because the Nazis considered us German, even though we'd never lived anywhere other than Yugoslavia. The ethnically Serbian and Croatian men, however, remained in town, and they were who we looked to as a way of keeping the bakery open. Father's cornbread, the kind he made for the Serbian bricklayers, had already established an easy rapport with our neighbors. Getting additional help was easy enough, but we never knew how long we'd have them, if and when they'd be swept up into the surrounding storm of war.

The town felt both full and empty at the same time. The streets were filled with strange faces and strange dialects. Of strange people waving their banners, red and black. It was a stark juxtaposition against the hemorrhage-like loss of fathers and brothers and friends, all of whom were forced to leave. It felt like one group of people had slowly replaced the other. And it made me angry. Made Mother boil.

"Those Germans," she'd hiss under her breath as she kneaded bread dough or went over the store's ledgers. None of us could truly grasp why this was happening. Local politicians spouted opinions, loudly in the main square or quietly in secret alleys, but mother didn't care, still didn't understand. She thought only of Father, of Henry, of the cottage in the country and everything that seemed to disappear the moment they left.

Jens: Dachau, 1942

There is a sickly smell that refuses to dissipate even as the morning sun breaks through the dark sky as I walk from my barracks to the bakery where I've been stationed. Charred and sallow, the clouds plume overhead, manufactured gray and white and black, inky as it unfurls.

My baker's hands move quickly to make light work. I have been making bread. So much bread. My fingers have blisters, are burned like the sky, charred and sallow like the smoke, as I lift loaf after loaf from the ovens. The bricks pile on top of each other, the pale yellow mortar binds the masonry, building up and out. This is a place with no limits, a world with no time, fenced in and parceled out according to a classification that no one knows.

I start counting the days by the leaves on the trees that surround the perimeter. Orange leaves wither and fall within three days; green leaves grow verdant and waxy for months, until they yellow into two days. Sweet buds, snowy and purple, are a blissful springful seven days. Bare branches, stocky and peeled, hold the days in a liminal vice that continues until I can no longer breathe. On cold days, my lungs threaten to pop as snow and sleet blanket the long grassy patches between the bricks. But before I feel like I might explode, the bark surrenders to the blooms and I begin to count again.

There is a winterly pallor over the pale purples of spring that never leaves entirely. It is accompanied by a noiseless scream that, even in its quietude, is heard throughout the camp. Its silence slinks its way through every barrack and pit. It embeds itself in my oven and my shovel and my skin. It takes me weeks to realize what I am smelling is death.

Chapter 7

The small bell twitched as Sera's boot kicked against the grocery store's front door, popping it open as it scraped against the doorway. The door had never sat quite flush against the door frame after Albert and Henry had taken up the task of doing some minor updates to the grocery store's facade.

To take a baker and put him in carpenter's clothes was a sight to see—the normally serene Albert, with his quiet confidence and singularly intuitive way in which he moved around the kitchen, became red-faced and fumbling. But this is what it meant to work with Father, to live with Father: none of us sat within a singular classification. I was a daughter, teacher, accountant, shelf-stocker, and occasional medical hobbyist, when Frankie skinned his knee and Mother was too busy negotiating with customers to tend to him. Albert was no exception, and when the door needed to be replaced, he found himself, hammer in hand, cursing at hinges that didn't quite match the pin. Or at least, that's what I assumed when, through the window, I saw him throw down the hardware, his fists clenched, his arms a fury of frustration, as he stormed off toward the lake. Albert, the consummate professional, who was steady and sure throughout the long, meticulous hours of mixing and kneading, pitching, and proofing, had met his match with the door frame.

A few centimeters above the floor, the paint was stripped bare. Mother and I always talked about fixing it, especially on hot days when the wood would swell and the door would stick so firmly that customers would have to use their shoulders to enter.

Today, the weather was cool, brisk enough that Sera's gentle kick made the door burst forward. A clash of scrapes and bells announced her arrival. With Father gone and with Mother managing the house and bakery, I ran the store mostly on my own. There were also days when my mother would slip out of the house early in the morning, before the store opened, and remove one of our best hams from the butcher case, slipping it into her bag alongside a loaf of hot bread. The first time I saw her do this, I was in shock, my mouth agape. Ham was expensive and hard to come by, even with a fresh month's worth of ration cards. But she told me to pay it no mind as the door scraped behind her.

"I swear, it's the grammar that drives me crazy." Sera sighed, her usual flair for dramatics elongating every syllable, her elbows resting on the store's counter as I tallied the leger from the night before. I smiled. In the midst of everything, knowing I could count on the ever-unchanging Sera felt like a connection to normalcy that I craved most days.

"I'm finding the more I practice, the less strange it feels. Honestly, for me it's the spelling," I replied, recollecting the previous night's German class and the vocabulary assignment we had to turn in. Even with high marks, I still felt like I couldn't quite grasp writing in German with the same fluidity I felt when

I spoke it.

One of my earliest lessons in German, before the Nazi occupation, was on the difference between the informal *du*, and the more formal *Sie*—one used when addressing dear friends, the other when speaking to strangers or work colleagues. Oma, my first German teacher, would speak to me softly (*verstehst du meine mausi?)* as I practiced telling her the colors and animals I had learned at John of Nepomuk. My earliest teacher, my earliest German, enshrouded in the gentleness of *du* and the safety of familiarity.

With the occupation, and the prevalence of German in our day-to-day lives, Anica, Sera, and I took night classes to improve our grammar and written German, two things that seemed increasingly essential as our encounters shifted into the language of our oppressors. In this world, *Sie* became the identifier, not only for those to whom we were speaking, but for the life we lived as soon as we stepped outside the safety of home: rigid, inflexible, and so very formal.

"Have you heard from either of them?" Sera's demeanor flickered from her usual lightness into one weighed down by unease.

"No. Nothing," I answered quietly. It had been months since Father and Henry had left. No correspondence had arrived. We tried to write, but our letters went unanswered. Mother never let herself show us any worry. She held her back straight, her gaze focused, as she organized each day's tasks and pilfered the occasional ham for her secret errands in town. Once in a while, as we readied ourselves for bed and switched from electric lights to gas lanterns, I'd catch a flicker of worried weariness as the light hit her face, only to disappear as the flame burned brighter.

Sera was silent for a moment, before bursting into a smile. "Let's go to the cinema tonight! A bit of a celebration since German class was canceled. There's no use sitting at home, worrying, no?"

I pressed my lips into a soft smile. Sera was right: movies were a good distraction. Even though they only showed German war films, we were far enough removed from the front that what we saw on the screen was still an escape from reality. I couldn't imagine Father with his gray hair, Henry with his boyish grin, or Albert with his soft baker hands, red with oven burns, running through barbed wire or dodging artillery shells.

◆◆◆◆

Mother's eyes glittered as she moved around the kitchen, cooking up a small parcel of sausage she'd been saving in the icebox. To all our delight, Father sat at the table with us, laughing. Mother blushed with happiness.

The night before, as I was going over orders for the store, I heard the door scrape against the swollen wood in chorus with the tinny ring of the bell.

"We're closed," I said, my eyes still fixed on the forms that sat on the counter as I tallied how much cabbage we'd need to get at the market later that week.

By this point, I was used to customers both underestimating and undermining me. Father had trained me well to operate all aspects of the store, but my youthful face led others to assume I wasn't capable of running the business without him. Any sweetness or shyness had already transformed into something more surly and hardened with the arrival of the Germans and now, as the unofficial proprietress of the store, I bristled easily at any perceived implication that I wasn't capable. Like this lingering customer who seemed to ignore that I had closed for the evening.

"Please, we're clos—"

My reproach turned into a gasp and evolved rapidly into a yelp as I rushed around the till and landed into the open arms of my father.

A little thinner, the gray whisps on his temple more pronounced, I could tell that even six months in, the army had already aged him. But in the crush of his army wools, he still smelled like Father.

When he walked into the house, Mother cried. We hadn't received any news: we didn't know where they were, what had happened after basic training, if they had been deployed to different countries, if they were fighting on different fronts. The only thing we knew was that they were still alive, somewhere, but even then, we had learned quickly that to be alive could mean a wide range of things, some of which were no better than death.

As the dry leaves danced along the gray cobblestoned streets, the trees bare in our eternal winter, I wondered if Henry still practiced his accordion fingerings on pieces of cardboard, like he did before we went to the teachers college in Werschetz. Or if Father remembered how to make my favorite little cakes, Mladenčići, sweet honey rolls that our Serbian customers bought for weddings. When I was young, my father always said that barely touching the dough and letting the ingredients combine almost intuitively was what made them so light and delicious. This was the alchemy of baking, the magic, he told me. The beauty of the yeast knowing when to bubble and flour understanding when to rise. When the dough, rough and crumbling, was smoothed out by father's quick and gentle kneads, he'd wink at me, peering over the edge of the counter.

"You only need to listen, Else. The dough always tells you what it needs."

And now, as he sat at the kitchen table, a spread of all the little delicacies Mother kept tucked away now in front of him—salted butter, homemade jam, the sausages she'd been saving for a special occasion—Father told us that he had been assigned to baking duty at a training camp just north of Munich, a former German munitions factory they called Dachau. I heard mother humming as she moved around the kitchen, giving Joshi and Frankie instruction on the chores that needed to happen after lessons.

The sunlight streaming through the window, the rhythm we'd established as a family truncated by war, all of it was buoyed by a lightness we hadn't felt in months. Everything was the same, and yet, nothing was, as Father recounted tales of basic training and early assignment. The unexpected joy of seeing him sit at our table also meant that soon, we could hope to see Henry, perhaps also without warning but with dizzying anticipation.

"Mausi, you wouldn't believe how much bread we make," he told me as I sat down, readying myself for a day at the store. I couldn't help but smile—he hadn't called me by my childhood nickname since I graduated with my *Abitur*, and like the butter, it also felt like a treat.

"I tell you, the German army must only be fueled by brown bread at the rate we're making loaves. That, and cigarettes," he said, sipping his coffee before slapping his knees and standing up.

"Shall I come with you to the store this morning, Else? Your mother tells me you've been running a well-organized operation in my absence."

Chapter 8

Father's visit eight months ago had left us with a renewed sense of levity that, while it slowly dissipated as the days lengthened into the weeks and months from that first morning he sat in the kitchen, had also lingered as a reminder of what had been.

A more lasting remnant of father's brief visit home was Mother's growing pregnant belly. New life in the midst of loss, while a joyful distraction, also felt unnatural. Without Father, without Henry, there was no immediate sense of celebration. I wondered if we'd know how to welcome a new baby into our family. If a world of withouts could hold the hope of new life.

It was still dark when mother woke me up, slowly leading me into the kitchen as she braced herself against the wall with her right hand. "Else, I need you to make sure Joshi and Frankie make it to school in the morning."

Mother lowered herself slowly onto a kitchen chair, wincing. Her left hand cradled her belly as her right dabbed her brow with her handkerchief, both now wet with perspiration. It was late, the moonless sky darker than usual.

"Mother, I should stay with you." I looked at the clock, wondering if I should rouse Mary who would be waking soon in order to head into town for work. Could she stay behind to help with the boys?

Months earlier, after my father left, she tried to shield her sickness from us and the fatigue that seemed to set in early in the afternoons, just as the boys came home from school. Mary would shuffle them into the store, where they did their schoolwork next to me at the till, while she helped with dinner. Mother would move food around her plate, in an attempt to hide her diminished appetite.

One afternoon, after closing the store for the midday meal, I found my mother at the table, head in hand, her cheeks wet. As soon as she saw me, she straightened her back and mustered a small smile.

"Well, my dearest girl. It seems as though there will be another one of us in a few short months."

I thought of the store's ledgers, how they reflected ration books and very little profit, of the banners that now streamed down the sides of municipal buildings, red and black and strange. I thought of Father so very far away and the uncertainty we lived with day to day. I thought these things, and in her eyes, I saw that she thought them too. So I leaned into her, wrapping my arms around her hunched shoulders.

"How wonderful. How so very wonderful."

And now, seven months later, we sat at the same table, Mother cradling her head again, this time her breath stilted and labored.

"Get some sleep Else," she muttered as the quietness of night lay heavy in the kitchen, her hand gripping mine. I sat, unmoving, stroking my thumb against her palm, rubbing her back as the contractions intensified.

As the early morning light streamed through the windows, my mother screamed. Dawn cracked the sky open into blushed blues and oranges as my mother's body shook against the new day.

"You need to get up," I whispered to Mary. "I think mother's about to give birth and I need to get the midwife." Her eyes bleary and still heavy with sleep, Mary turned to grab the clothes she had laid out the night before.

"No, there's no time," I hushed, rushing her out of the room into the kitchen. As soon as she saw mother, her eyes widened. Now fully awake, Mary took my place at the table as I slipped my coat on and left.

The grayness of the early morning made the air hazy, the path clouded by the graininess of a sun not yet fully risen.

The midwife lived on the other side of town, normally a twenty-minute stroll, but that morning I made it in what felt like just a few minutes. Breathless, I rapped the front door as any concern for early morning impropriety evaporated. She arrived at the door with the same degree of bleariness I had recognized in Mary in what had felt like minutes earlier.

"My mother," I gasped. "My mother needs you. I think the baby is coming soon."

The midwife nodded silently, holding her hand up to show she understood, then turned slowly back into the house.

I leaned my body into the doorway. "Did you hear me?" I whispered. "I said I think the baby's coming soon." She turned and raised her index finger, still nodding her head and beckoned me inside.

The sun was growing larger in the sky, the urgency of the matter felt palpable and yet, as I watched the midwife kneel to pray, my chest constricted with the fear that perhaps she didn't feel the same sense of immediacy.

But what to do with a woman in prayer? I silently recited a string of "Hail Marys," hoping that time would both speed up and stand still. And that Mary wouldn't have to deliver a baby on our kitchen floor.

In the warmth of a new day, we welcomed our littlest brother. Pink and small, his head covered in fine hairs, dark brown just like Father's, his body curled against Mother's as he yelped his first cry, establishing his tiny but significant existence. Our sweet Mathias, born into a world not of our making but already bravely making his voice heard.

◆◆◆◆

To live within the passage of time, to really understand the movement of the days, I had to experience the sunrise and sunset with new life; a baby developing and growing more rapidly than a calendar could ever hold.

Sweet Mathias, with his cry, woke us up to the days—no longer were we settled in the liminal space of grayness, but now were fully alive, attending to his every need while we kept the shop running and the bakery ovens hot. Mother would keep him in a small basket on the floor of the kitchen while we prepared for the day, Mary stopping every few minutes to wiggle her fingers across his face, making his tiny nose scrunch and his blue eyes, big and limitless, blink.

Joshi and Frankie were, at first, mystified by Mathias's smallness, the way his tiny fingers would wrap around their thumbs as he slept, his eyelids nearly translucent, stippled by a pattern of small, thin blood vessels. They sat on their heels, looking down at him, then at each other, then at Mother, until she told him that they could gently touch his hand or sweetly brush his soft forehead with their palms. When they both realized that this was the extent of the fun they'd be able to have with their new brother until he could keep his eyes open a bit longer, they ran out of the kitchen and into the living room where we could hear them wrestle.

As the floorboards reverberated with loud thuds, body slams punctuated by fits of giggling and the occasional yelp, Mother looked over the store's inventory, a ritual we'd formed in the early hours of the day while we prepared little boys for their lessons and ourselves for business.

Mother ran her finger down the list, pausing at the section that accounted for the butcher case. Without a butcher, and in the midst of wartime occupation, we rarely sold fresh meat and instead filled the shelves with anything that was cured or smoked. The selection was sparse and whatever we could get at the market, no matter how measly or anemic, was expensive. Our stomachs were filled with milk and bread, potatoes and cabbage. Small portions of butter were rationed for special days; meat was saved for meager celebrations.

Her finger paused on the list, lingering over an item that had been written with careful precision: *der schinken.* Ham. We only had a few left and of the lot, we carved them into small portions to be doled out when customers extended their stamp, precious and dear, guarded only for the most auspicious of occasions.

"Else, bring one back to the house when you close up the shop tonight," she said, as if an afterthought, before quickly moving to Mathias as he started to wake.

It had been two months since the midwife, fresh from morning prayers, had delivered Mathias into the world, and at least three since mother had requested ham from the store's limited stock.

My head whipped over my shoulder to where she was bending down to pick up Mathias.

"Mother."

She nuzzled her face into the baby's downy hair fuzz, closing her eyes as she breathed deeply.

"Else, please," she breathed, the fatigued voice of a mother in early babyhood. Her lips curled into a smile as she swayed my littlest brother, her apron fluttering with the morning breeze. Her eyes opened and looked into mine. They were soft, but strong. A tired resolution. She looked back down at the baby, then kissed his head before placing him in my arms.

"We do what we need to do." Her voice trailed in a whisper before she adjusted her apron strings then winked at me and took back Mathias. "Just don't forget to bring the ham home tonight, yes?"

I nodded and made a note in the ledger. One whole ham, nearly a ration's book of meat, removed from the store's shelves. There was a part of me that hated not knowing what mother was up to, that the secret whispers that had become a hallmark of occupation were permeating our home. But there was also the counter, the gentle nudge of reflection that transcended any anger or frustration: mother knew how to survive, or at the very least, what it took to make it through the long days and nights without folding into herself. Other women had grown pale with anxiety, the weight of the unknown wearing on their bodies as they grieved for lost husbands, lost sons, lost livelihoods. But Mother had kept her buoyancy in a way that kept the rest of us above water. Perhaps it was the ham.

Years later, I found out what the hams were for; how they had been used to sweeten our sour situation, not quite a bribe, but gifts in good faith that ultimately resulted in our father's homecoming a year after Mathias was born in 1943. Instead of being forced to enlist in another term of active duty, he was released. Turned out that even people in power hungered for the deliciousness of a previous life, where abundance replaced the ever-present scarcity of 1940s Betschkerck.

With Father back, our wartime routine, which had become normal in its abnormality, shifted again. He resumed his roles as baker and grocery store manager with such ease, it almost felt like he'd never left. But I could tell that he crossed our threshold a changed man, if only by the quietness with which he sat at the table before dinner each night, lost in thought.

"Lissie, I could tell something wasn't right." I heard him speaking in low tones as I rushed into the house, late from a shift at my new job at the courthouse issuing travel permits. Often, I'd linger and talk with Anica and Sera, who had also gotten jobs in the same office. Traveling beyond town limits was prohibited, unless you had a permit—another unwanted change brought by the occupation.

"I guess I'm lucky that I didn't see any real combat as an army baker, but...." His voice trailed. "There's something wrong going on over there, I know it. Even the sky never seems to change from gray to blue." He paused and shifted his eyes to the floor. "The smell, Lissie. The smell never leaves. It burned the inside of my nose like it was sour. Almost like I was inhaling death."

Chapter 9

It was a good year. Or rather, 1943 was the kind of year that, if you squinted your eyes just a bit and blurred out the Nazi insignia that surrounded the town square, and furrowed your brow to forget that Henry was still in the German army, life felt like it hummed along the current that flowed around us before the occupation.

There were differences, of course; the most pronounced were the hardest to ignore. Our Jewish neighbors were gone, their storefronts either empty or filled with new businesses that felt like a paled reflection of the vibrancy the previous establishments had offered. Daily, friends and acquaintances seemed to leave or disappear and the lively hum of Betschkerck evaporated without so much as a whimper.

With father back and able to run the bakery and grocery store with mother, I decided to accept a promotion as a court reporter at another courthouse that had just been built. For 7000 Dinars a month, a modest if not good salary, I sat in a beautiful building and transcribed misdemeanor cases, mostly petty crime like the occasional theft. It was another layer to this facade of normalcy that we had created with father's return; the elegant struggle of occupation melting away with everyday offenses like shoplifting or drinking too many mugs of ale and relieving yourself on the steps of the town hall before wobbling home.

I loved it all—the distraction of the unsavory, but relatively harmless, the rigid schedule, money I was able to bring home. Each morning as I put on my jacket, a smart black wool coat in the winter, a camel-colored macintosh in the cooler fall months, I'd find myself slipping into the daydream of the life I was living, continuing and stretching into the months and years to come.

It's not that I relished the thought of this strange new world lingering into the evening song of my adulthood, but to live for even a moment without the trepidation of constant change or ceaseless unfamiliarity felt like a brief respite. A gift. But each morning, as I walked through the main square and passed Mr. Zalabak's old storefront, the red paint nearly chipped away but still a stain on the Jewish bakery's window, I'd see the old baker's eyes as they reflected the sharp angles and unforgiving forms of circumstance, one that had never left but morphed itself into something softer but altogether deceiving. We lived our lives as though stability had finally been achieved but scarcity continued to dictate our days and we hadn't seen Mr. Zalabak in years.

But as I pulled on my gloves and closed the door behind me and began my walk to the courthouse I couldn't suppress the sweetness of joyfully living. Yes, there was pain and uncertainty, and oh how I missed Henry. But here, on the cusp of adulthood, it felt as though my feet had finally found the sureness of steady ground, even if I didn't fully realize that I was standing on a sinkhole.

Chapter 10

The knock on the window was loud enough to wake the house and early enough that the blushed pink of the new day had only just begun to crack through the night sky.

This is what I remember: voices that were both hushed and intrusive, my mother's reaction to an urgent whisper that panicked against her steady responses.

She roused us from our beds, already half-awake from the disruption, and gave quick instruction. As I pulled my dress over my head, her words came fast, but steady:

"Pack as many good clothes as you can into a suitcase. Don't forget a blanket and pillow."

"Else, when you're done, go to the store with Father and pull enough bread, ham, salt, and sugar to fill two sacks—but not too heavy. I don't know how long we'll have to carry everything."

"Mary, get me my sewing kit. Hurry."

Mother sat at the kitchen table, ripping open the lining of her winter coat, a soft satin that frayed against the violence of each seam tear. In front of her, three piles of paper money. Without looking up, she called me over.

"Else, have you packed your suitcase."

I nodded, pulling another heavy sweater over my head.

"I need you to put this with your things," she whispered, lifting her head, handing me one of the stacks, a handful of dinars.

"Keep your suitcase as close to you as possible. Don't let it out of your sight. If something happens and we get separated, use the money to find food or a place to stay or find transportation that's going in the direction of Germany."

She started portioning out a second stack of bills, putting the smaller sections against the wool of the coat, positioning them so they sat flush with the corner seam without protruding out. Carefully laying the now-damaged lining against the coat, the dinars disappeared under a layer of satin.

Her stitches were quick and fast and before long, she was pulling her hands through the arms of the coat, buttoning it up to her chin. She tugged on the cuffs and smoothed down the front and, placing her hands on my shoulders, she leaned her head close to mine.

"Your father is going to put the rest of the money in his suitcase. Between the three of us, we have 300,000 dinars." Her voice was still hushed, but steady. Breathless, but defiant. It was the most money I'd ever seen. Mother must have taken everything we had from the bank, from the bakery and grocery store tills—our life's savings, now sewn into coat linings and tucked into suitcases, beneath undergarments.

We moved so quickly around the apartment, even in our silence well choreographed. It was as though the months and years of trepidation and quiet fear had given us a language for survival, direct but unspoken.

The rap at the window had told us this much: the Russian military was invading Yugoslavia, crowding in on Betschkerck. Anyone who was of German descent was at risk for being jailed or sent to a labor camp, undeserved retribution for the sins of our occupiers. Mother had already heard rumors about some of our cousins who had been captured by the Russians. They were forced to work in the coal mines where they were mentally and sexually tortured.

We moved so quickly we couldn't think, assembling packages in anticipation for the unknown. Within an hour we had forty parcels filled with two accordions, a radio, and the bread, ham, salt, and sugar I had helped father procure from the store. We each had a suitcase packed with warm clothes, my winter coat shoved between socks and an extra pair of boots, the Dinars hidden in a pair of nylon stockings stuffed into a side pocket, sewn into the interior.

In the front hall of our house, as mother took an assessment of what we had, the four older children stood waiting for her to give us a sharp nod—the kind of nod Mary and I had learned to anticipate in early childhood after morning chores, or before morning mass, our dresses smartly pressed and ribbons cleanly tied. A nod that signaled correctness and completion; the anticipation of expectation achieved. And yet, in the early hours of the day, we didn't know the goal of our task. To leave, yes, but to go where? And for how long? Perhaps her nod of affirmation would imbue the dusky filled morning with a thread of comfort.

I shifted weight from foot to foot, left to right, swaying in rhythm with the mid-autumn wind that rustled the drying leaves. My blood tingled with unplaced adrenaline as my body leaned into the weight of a sleepless stupor, the exhaustion of the morning threatening to wrap us numb. I fixed my eyes on the plaster wall in front of us, on a spot stained with water spots, chipped from where the outside door hit the inner wall. It held our hurried returns from school in the cold, dark short days of winter; the afternoon Anica, Sera, and I got caught in an early summer storm after laying on the banks of Bega Lake when Anica told us she had finally kissed the sweet Serbian baker's son; the first night I came home after Henry and father had left for the army and the emptiness that welcomed me at the door. I leaned forward, across the hall to touch the rough edges of its uneven texture and wished I could kiss it.

Mother zipped the final suitcase and straightened up. Her nod was sharp enough for me to trust her; stilted enough for me to understand that trust now meant something different. Father rushed into the foyer with a bundle, wrapped in an old scarf. He held it out to us before burying it in another package.

"Watches. For selling or bartering if we need food." His voice was hushed, even though we lived on the outskirts of town, away from any lingering ears and eyes.

We stood in silence as the morning, streaked with orange, filtered through the window in the door, washing us in golden light. The chipped plaster wall glittered in the day's new sun. In the distance, an owl called to another, harkening its early morning hunt.

I looked at the clock and closed my eyes to etch the time in my memory. *Seven o'clock. October 2, 1944. A Monday.* The floorboards groaned as we shifted our weight. *Seven o'clock.* I thought of the lace curtains in the kitchen. *October 2.* The forget-me-knots on my bed's coverlet. *Seven o'clock.* A chipped dish in the cupboard. *October 2.* The way the meadow sang in the early summer morning. *Seven o'clock.*

Seven o'clock. Seven o'clock. Seven o'clock.

And then, we left.

SZIGETI E
SZÁLLITÓ
SZEKSZÁRD

Anna Meyer: Tschetereg 1944

The water from an old pipe drips down the wall, streaking the ruddy bricks of the old schoolhouse. She wants to lick the walls, her thirst overcoming any sense of decency. She lays on the floor, on her back, the straw sticking out of the threadbare mattress cover, scratching her skin, bruised and blue.

Her tongue is sticky as she runs it around the edges of her mouth, cracked and bleeding. The schoolhouse is as familiar as the flowers that grow outside of her childhood home. But the bricks give no comfort. She has tried counting them, first starting from the corner, then from the ceiling, then from the middle of the floor, counting each brick as if she were collecting them, as if knowing their number would release her from these walls.

It has been days since she's had any food, any water. Light shines in from the windows from where she can see a small patch of blue speckled with dust, white and gray and small. And flowers. There are also flowers, the kind that grew outside her house. She attempts to smile, her lips crack. She wonders what it would be like to pick them right now, to gather them in her apron. But she can't lift them into her palms; she cannot bury her face in their perfume like she did when she was younger.

She is so hungry. She imagines eating the flowers. They would taste like clouds that pierce the blueness that surrounds her.

Instead, she tastes dirt and shit and straw and scratch. She cannot stop licking the floor, imagining what it would be like to savor the flowers.

It is gray, then black, then gray, then light and she wakes, her cheek pressed against the straw mattress, the blue sky faded into a purplish black. She hears breathing, heavy and sporadic. She hears silence, deafening and still. They've moved the bodies, stiff and sallow, to the sides of the room. First Grandmother, then Grandfather. Then Mother. Sister. Sister. Sister. Cousin. Friend. In the center of the room, she listens to the void as her father scratches at the sky.

"Water," she hears a voice say before it's enveloped in boots and voices and Козёл! Засранец! Козёл! Засранец! Козёл! Засранец! Козёл! Засранец!

"Water, water everywhere" the voice says. "And nor a drop to drink."

Chapter 11

We arrived as the sun was just starting to crest over the bare branches of the forest that surrounded Bega Lake. Just outside of the clearing, where the grass grew flat to the ground as it sloped into the lake, unfurling in a tide of reeds and rushes that poked out of waters greenish brown, an open truck sat idling. The smell of diesel mixed with the musky smell of algae while the truck's owner, Mr. Petrović, leaned against it and picked at his teeth with his pinky nail.

By the time we had crossed the field in front of our home and made our way through the wooded path that led to the lake, a group of neighbors had gathered. Like us, they held suitcases filled with packages, coats tightly wrapped around their middles, scarves tightly knotted under chins. I wondered, as I gripped my suitcase handle harder, how many thousands of dinars were sewn into the linings of coats and parcels, and if they also took inventory of their valuables, not to keep safe, but to determine which would buy them passage to safety.

Mr. Petrović adjusted his posture and started walking toward us. His voice was hushed as we gathered close.

"Is this all of you?"

I looked around me, a small sea of familiarity; faces and names of friends with last names like Müller and Weber; people, like us, whose tongues rolled with the gentle current of Serbian as it ebbed and flowed in our mouths, tripping over the guttural, less natural German of our imposed heritage. Germans by blood only—but blood was all it took.

No one said anything and yet, that was enough for each of us, one by one, to step into the flatbed of the truck. I pressed myself against the railing to make room for the others. Below me, just next to the truck, Bega Lake. The surface was still, like glass, reflecting in nearly perfect composition the trees that surrounded the water. Their leaves, an almost fantastical blend of reds and yellows, reminded me of Tschetereg, of the sweetness of childhood. But like the reflection, I knew that my memories were only mirrored copies of the originals—nearly the same, but not quite. Similar enough to tempt me with a longing for the sweetness of youth, before the Russians, before the occupation, before Lake Bega, now still and serene, pulled me under. When German was only my schoolhouse language.

The truck was small enough that our twenty-some bodies pressed against each other and jostled violently with each turn. It only took an hour to cross the bridge that spanned Lake Bega and brought us over the Yugoslavian-Hungarian border. But the light felt different—a brighter sun compared to the softness of the early morning, but also, perhaps a sun different from the one we left. This, a Hungarian sun that reflected off the Hungarian bricks that built the Hungarian train station. The light felt different perhaps because it reflected off spaces and bodies—our own bodies—now so foreign from what we had known. In the span of a few hours, we had gone from being Yugoslavian bakers to German refugees, carrying bags of sugar and salt.

Except, there was no sugar. Or salt. As the truck rattled toward the train station, we made quick inventory of the packages we had loaded into the truck. Mother was carrying Mathais, now two. Normally he squirmed whenever she held him close, but this morning he slept, his head heavy against her shoulder. She shifted him from one shoulder to the other, her knees bending under the weight of his body as she moved him. Mary, small enough to crouch down between the crowded feet, opened each bag. Joshi and I pressed against her, trying to create some kind of barrier, to protect her from the rogue knees or foot stamps that accompanied each truck jostle.

She tugged at the hem of my jacket.

"Else," Mary whispered. "I need you."

I bent down, suddenly in the cocoon of legs, a strange, quieted space of tranquility after what felt like hours of an abrasive combination of diesel and wind.

"Who took the sugar?" I could feel her breath on my cheek.

"I thought you did. Or Father?"

"We split the bags, but I took most of it since I had the most space—" Mary went silent. "It's all gone."

My hands brushed over each package with urgency. In wartime, salt and sugar were more valuable than paper money. With it, we'd have a reliable way of bartering and securing food or lodging; without it, we were at the mercy of strangers. And if the occupation had taught us anything, compassion seemed to be in short supply.

The truck lurched to a stop, throwing us forward. I heard muffled shouting from Mr. Petrović and Joshi pulled Mary and me back up.

"We're in Hungary," he leaned forward to whisper. "We need to get out of the truck."

The bodies around us moved and shifted, the energy still anxious with the unknown.

"But the sugar," Mary began to bend over her bag. I grabbed her shoulders as people pushed past us.

"We can't worry about that now." I guided her off the truck, my grip firm. Her eyes filled with tears as she adjusted the buttons on her coat, hoisting her bag onto her back. I could sense her resignation, but knew it was tinged with regret. Perhaps not regret, but the misplaced determination to make it right. To find the lost bags of salt and sugar. To return to Yugoslavia. It was more than losing something valuable—it was a recognition of vulnerability. Without sugar, what could we offer? Without Yugoslavia, who were we?

"I just—" Mary lifted her head, locking eyes with me. She pressed her lips together. "I just..."

I'll always remember her eyes in that moment: a glassy blue, glazed with fresh tears.

The sun had risen, illuminating a sky that mirrored the color of my sister's eyes. A gust of wind blew across my face; my curled hair moving with it. The air smelled of burnt leaves and freshly dewed grass, an amalgamation of late summer and early fall.

And then sulfur. And fire. And noise.

My teeth slammed together as the earth shook. My jaw clamped against the sound of screaming metal.

In the distance we saw smoke, a plume rising from where the bridge over Bega Lake met its Hungarian shore and then a B-24, flying near the ground before ascending quickly.

No sooner had we made it across the water, the bridge that had delivered us safely was bombed. A few kilometers away, our bags unloaded and piled against the wall of the train station we were only close enough to taste the smoke without experiencing the fullness of the explosion. But there still lingered a sense of hope enshrouded within a new kind of fear that was beginning to unfold—a new sense of exposure that came with being a person with no country. A family with no home.

We realized immediately something that we held onto for the rest of our lives. That if we had been a moment too soon, or a moment too late, we would have evaporated with the smoke, or worse, been left in Yugoslavia.

Years later, as the fog of war finally lifted and we tried to make sense of what we left behind, we learned that our Uncle Martin Meyer, our mother's brother, and his family, along with our maternal grandparents, were locked in a school room after their town was invaded by the Russian army, and starved to death.

Only 30 kilometers from Betschkerck, their town was small but lively, a place that harkened us with long nights of story and song. And our grandmother's beef goulash that tasted almost like Mother's, but was just different enough that we couldn't help ourselves but to eat seconds, and thirds, and sometimes, even—if you were Frankie—fourths. Each time I asked how she made it, what she did differently, she'd wink before holding her index finger against her pressed lips.

"Soon enough, sweet Else," she'd coo before rushing us out of the kitchen.

Mother had tried to convince them to come with us, but they couldn't understand leaving home. They trusted what they knew, and it killed them. Like most memories of the war, we held their death within the duality of pain: deep grief and deep guilt woven together, a rope of sorrow stretched across our hearts.

What did it feel like to learn, years later, that the only thing that kept us from a mass grave in the lush forests of Yugoslavia was a bridge over Bega Lake? It made me wish that the waters that tried to eat me had swallowed me whole.

Chapter 12

From the moment that Mathias was born, his rosy cheeks begged us to pinch them. His sweet smile seemed to grow bigger than his face as he toddled around the house, shrieking with laughter as he tried to keep up with Frankie, who relished no longer being the youngest and took pleasure in sneaking Mathias pieces of cake and soft bits of bread when Mother wasn't looking.

Perhaps we doted on him because he was the youngest, or perhaps it was his blue eyes, icy and calm, that held us in the palm of his doughy little hand. Of all of us, his eyes were the most arresting. "Eyes of a wartime baby," my mother would coo, nestling her face into his sweet baby neck rolls. What that meant, I didn't know, only that he was special—a lightness in the midst of such heaviness, with blue eyes buoyant enough to distract us from an ever-present sadness. But now, in Hungary, his eyes had dulled, his cheeks were pale.

After the smoke had cleared from the bombing, German soldiers arrived with another truck that took us to a local school.

"There's space for you in the main hall," the young lieutenant told us, pointing toward the doors as we stepped out of the flatbed. An old janitor greeted us at the door. With quick, jerking motions, pulled his fingers close to his face. Father walked over and we watched them speak in hushed tones, each using broad hand signals to communicate their ideas. We spoke Serbian, German, a little bit of French, but surely no Hungarian. At least not enough to ask what I was sure we were all thinking:

"Where are we? And where are we going? And how did we get here?"

What will happen next?

It took Father only three steps to return to our group, his strides wide and full of energy. I could tell that the stress of our quick departure from home had been replaced with adrenaline—a low, gentle hum that glowed behind his slate blue eyes that mimicked the way they twinkled on those cold mornings in December when he made *božićna* kolač, Serbian Christmas bread for our neighbors. When I was younger, he'd let me pick out a gold coin from the till drawer to bake into the bread, a token of prosperity for whomever found it in their piece.

"But where will I find all the good luck for this bread, Else?" he'd muse out loud.

"From me, Papa!" I'd giggle, slowly revealing the cent piece in my hand. His gasp would send me into fits of laughter, which melted into a sweet youthful pride I'd carry with me throughout the day. I fancied myself a mistress of luck and fortune, skipping to class through the snowdrifts.

But here in Hungary, we were bereft of the good fortune I once imagined I brought to our Christmas time customers. Instead of gold coins, we craved the comfort of a warm bed.

"The Germans have taken over transportation, laws, and any kind of regulations," Father seemed to tell us everything in one breath. "There is no food here, or water, so we'll have to rely on what we have for the time being. But the school is warm, or at the very least dry. The old man said as long as people behave, they're left more or less alone."

He clapped his hands together, rubbing them to keep warm. Mary let out a quiet sob.

"The salt...." she whispered, before burying her head in her hands. I fit my arm around her shoulders and pulled her into my chest. Father leaned close.

"Mary, dear, what...why are you crying?" His voice was soft and concerned.

"The salt...the sugar..." she said in small heaves of breath, "... gone."

Father pulled her away from me, into his arms.

"Shhhhhhh," he said, quieting her. "It's okay. We'll be okay." I saw his eyes lift toward Mother's as she shook her head ever so slightly. I saw his body fall into a sigh.

Once inside the school, we were able to finally take inventory of what we had brought from Betschkerck. The provisions were laid out, everything that we had stuffed into worn bags. The Dinars stayed clumsily sewn into coat linings and suitcase pockets. While we had lost most of the sugar and salt, we still had the watches, the accordions, and the money that had been divided amongst Father, Mother, and me.

"This should put us in a good position for bartering," Father murmured. We were standing so close to each other that our foreheads touched. The room was crowded and we didn't know who we could trust. We only knew that we needed to act smartly and efficiently.

"Where are we going?" Mary whispered, still pale with teenage remorse.

"I'm not sure," Father responded, looking over his shoulder. We were in the main dining room, a large open space that was filled with families like ours—people who had left their homes quickly, with little warning. Someone had pushed the tables to the edges of the room so that we could lay down coats and blankets to create makeshift beds. We had only what we brought with us. I saw a woman slicing a loaf of bread and made a note to see if we had extra ham to make a trade.

Mother was bouncing Mathias. His skin had grown more pale, now almost a sallow gray that glistened with fever. Normally a sweet, quiet baby, sensitive to noise, his lethargy made us worry.

One of the German soldiers, a sweet boy named Karl, had helped us find a doctor who immediately told Mother he had influenza.

"He barely looked at him," she muttered when she returned, Mathias both limp and fussy. She kissed his forehead and cooed in his ear, rubbing his back to make him more comfortable. I remembered how, when we were younger, she'd make us stay in bed and serve us lukewarm bowls of clear broth. Even when I was older, strong enough to lift the soup spoon on my own, I relished the moment when she'd tuck me in and slowly ladle the broth into my mouth. Even sick, I felt safe. I knew that Mother would nurse me back to health and that soon I'd be running to the lake with Sera and Anica.

I looked around the gray room that had been steadily filling with displaced families like ours. The coolness of a freshly changed bed and warm blankets were replaced with piles of threadbare linens and our mother's tired arms. She held Mathais and tilted her head up, toward mine.

"Can you see if someone has broth? Maybe ask one of the soldiers if they can get us some?" She clasped her hand in mine, the other holding Mathias close to her body. I knew I wouldn't find broth, even with ham to trade, but I squeezed her calloused palm, released it, and walked toward the soldier standing sentinel just outside the room, already knowing what his answer would be.

The next morning, I went with Mother to another physician. Mathias had gotten worse and she was convinced the other doctor had been wrong.

"This isn't influenza, Else," she muttered through clenched teeth as we walked into town, Mathias bundled tightly beneath her coat.

The doctor diagnosed him with tetanus and gave him a shot. Too sick to wail, he pressed his small body into my mother as a single tear ran down his cheek.

◆◆◆◆

It was still dark when the German soldiers roused us from our makeshift beds and told us to pack our things. We could hear the rain hitting the roof of the school, relentless and ceaseless. I looked for extra blankets for Mathias. Frankie, Mary, and Joshi stuffed what we had back into our suitcases while I felt for the Dinars in the coat lining. Neither of the Hungarian doctors had allowed us to pay, but we brought some ham, insisting they take it. As I walked out of the school into the rain, I was grateful to be free of the extra ham, even if its weight was paltry in comparison to, say, the accordions we had managed to hold onto.

We walked for fifteen minutes, back to the train station where a train sat, waiting for us. The cars were open freight, already filled with hundreds of other people, with no shelter from the weather.

We pressed in, Mother and Mathias going into the crowded train first so that they could be insulated from the rain as best as we could manage. Then me, then Mary, followed by the boys and finally, Father. My coat was already soaked through before the train started moving.

The night before, news had circulated that we were going to be moved from Hungary into Austria, a twelve-day journey. We assessed what we had, what we'd need, collecting bits of food and scarves to make the journey more manageable. Mother was still focused on Mathais. She smoothed his hair as he cried and changed his clothes when they got too damp from the fever, which still hadn't broken.

The rain was relentless, like shards of glass piercing any skin left exposed. Mathias had stopped crying, his body limp and his eyes like glass. Mother curved her back over him to try and keep him dry, but it was useless. Even with the rain, his fever ran hot.

I didn't remember falling asleep, but I remember Mother's shriek ripping through the wet darkness, rain still falling in sheets. I felt her body collapse to the floor of the train, moving the bodies around her like a ripple as we staggered against each other. I clasped Mary's shoulder as I moved, feeling not only the force of body against body, but the sharp wave of grief that Mother had released.

Just as I heard Mathias' first cries as the early morning light streamed into our small kitchen in Betschkerck, I now saw his limp body, still; life snuffed out by sickness and rain.

Lissie: Train, 1944

I cannot hear the conductor as he kneels in front of me, the rain dripping off the brim of his cap. I cannot hear anything but the rush of water. I feel my heart beating in my ears as heat flashes through my body. My arms are numb, but I cannot move them. My baby. My sweet baby boy. His eyes are still blue and I cannot bear it, but I cannot move my arms to free my hands to close his eyelids. His sweet precious eyelids. The conductor leaves, swallowed up by the wall of legs that surround me.

My husband holds my head in his arms, pulls my ear to his lips. He tells me to hold onto my baby, my sweet baby boy. To cover him with a blanket, to pretend he's not dead. My baby, my sweet baby boy. If I don't pretend, they'll take him now, he tells me. If I pretend, the Red Cross will bury him when we get to the next stop. But if I wrap him in a blanket, I won't see his beautiful blue eyes. They pierce my heart, his eyes. They ask me why I couldn't save him and I deserve to have them pin me in place, but Jens places my shawl over his face.

My arms are numb. And my body is numb. And my mind is numb. There are only legs and rain and brief moments when I dream and my baby, my sweet baby, is still alive. But I wake, and he is cold in my arms. There is rain and more rain and rain that feels like it will never end until it does. Or the train stops. I cannot tell, only that we are still and that there is a quiet and then, a silent parting of the legs.

A path is formed, at the end of which is a woman in a uniform. She asks for my baby, my sweet baby boy, and I hold him tighter. Her eyes are kind, but she tries again to take my baby, my sweet baby boy, and I try to tell her that I will hold him forever, that my arms are numb but that I am his mother and I must protect him, even now. I tell her this in low moans that push through my throat from a pit of sorrow deep within my body.

Jens holds me, kisses my hair, and tells me it's time. My baby, my sweet baby boy. He inserts his fingers into the creases between me and Mathias, gently pulling him out of my embrace. It is like when he was born, the midwife pulling him from my womb, the pain cutting like a knife. My arms burn as he is swallowed by the wall of legs. My baby. My sweet baby boy.

Chapter 13

What is time after loss? A long, unending stream of fog and rain, sun breaking through the clouds, the smell of sulfur and shit and earth as minutes and seconds press into each other. Mother's eyes were glass as she stared at the fields that rushed past us. Father had aged in the short time we had spent on the train, the wrinkles around his eyes deep with mourning. We gave the rest of our salt to the Red Cross, a token of gratitude for burying Mathias. We didn't know where he would be buried, only that it would be done properly. That sliver of humanity meant something.

◆ ◆ ◆ ◆

I don't remember how many days it took us to reach Kirchberg, an Austrian town in the eastern part of the country, nestled in the rolling hills of Brixental Valley. The air was cool when we stepped out of the freight car, the familiar crisp of autumn biting sharper still in the foothills of the mountains.

We silently stepped off the train in a single file line. Our family was muted by grief, but the fatigue that lingered among each family was palpable. At first, it had been impossible to sleep, the shock of cold air and rain kept us alert. But after a few days, after Mathias, it became too much. We'd lean on each other, my back against Mary's. Some days we'd take turns leaning against the wall of the train, sliding down to the floor, resting under the cover of bodies that broke the wind and sheltered us from the rain. Now that the train had stopped, now that we reached our next destination, all I could think about was lying down. My entire body was stiff, sore from standing for so many days.

We shuffled across the platform of the train station where three German soldiers were organizing us. A small crowd of Austrian men stood just beyond us, most wearing work clothes, silently sizing us up.

"As you know," one of the German soldiers began, his voice loud, "because you are German, you will be taken care of. We've asked our Austrian brothers and sisters to provide work and safe lodging for all of you and they have agreed to oblige."

I shifted my weight from one foot to the other, desperate for a bed. I rolled my head back, squinting into the sun before looking around at the crowd we were standing in, mostly men. Mostly young men or young families with only a baby or small child.

We later learned that the generous hospitality was a government mandate and that the Austrian men who had greeted us at the station were only looking for strong men to help with labor around their farms. Little by little, the crowd thinned until it was only the six of us standing on the platform. With two young women (me and Mary) and two small boys (Joshi and Frankie), we weren't useful. We'd take resources, like food, without giving much back.

"Else, I won't sleep at this train station," Mary whispered into my ear. I had been trying to stand a little straighter, trying to look pleasant and helpful as farmers from the town called forward other families and picked out pairs of bachelor brothers to help prepare the fields for the impending winter. I tried to look strong and dependable, knowing that whatever we could provide would ensure our survival. Mother was still pale, fragile with grief. And Frankie, newly ten, with his impish smile, made us seem less than reliable; I knew that I had to ignore the deep aches in my back and my sore legs and seem eager to work the land when all I craved was a warm bed and soft mattress.

We stood alone, the blue autumn light softening the lush green hillscape. I bent down to look inside my suitcase. We had given nearly all that was left of our salt to the man from the Red Cross. Most of our food was gone, eaten and bartered on the freight train. My face felt hot with fear and frustration as my throat swelled and tears filled my eyes. We had done what we were told, our father and brother had fought in the war, we had escaped the Russians, we had survived days and nights of cold rain in an open train, and now? Now we were abandoned in Austria, a family without a country, without a home. With no food or water.

"Hello?"

I looked up. The six of us shuffled slightly, as if moving as one unit, toward the voice. It belonged to a tall, thick man, with a gray beard and leathered skin. I could tell, with a glance, that he worked long hours outside, but his soft belly revealed that he enjoyed a more leisurely life than the farmers who had greeted us when we arrived.

"My name is Leopold Gruber." As he introduced himself, he walked toward where we were standing. His German, accented but familiar, reminded me that this place was familiar, yet foreign. Ah, how normal that feeling had become, the unease of everyday life. The mundanity of living had been replaced with the discomfort of survival, and here, in this sleepy Austrian town, Herr Gruber had extended his hand to our family.

That night, as we stood in a small square room, our shoulders touching, my eyelids heavy, I tried to listen to what he was telling us. His German wasn't our German, wasn't the soldier's German, but even in my haze of exhaustion I made an attempt to understand. Mother was still quiet and disconnected. Father looked as though he had aged ten years overnight. The heaviness of the coat, made heavier by the rain in the open freight car, had numbed my shoulders. My fingers played with the frayed edges of its sleeves.

"Well…." Herr Gruber picked at his nails. "This is what I have." He gestured around the room with his hand. His voice was tired, but kind. I wondered who he had said goodbye to, how the war had infiltrated the corners of his life.

"The room isn't very big, but it'll keep you warm. You'll have to share the space with Frau Bauer and her son—" he pointed to a small woman holding a young boy, around the age of six, who was standing near the door, "—but it should do."

We stood in silence. I tried to think of something to say but even gratitude felt forced. Our deep sadness made it difficult to think of anything other than home, or Mathias, or the sunlight, glittering on Lake Bega as I laughed with Anica and Sera.

Herr Gruber cleared his throat, shifting his body from side to side.

"I have a few vineyards that I'll need help with." He looked at Father. I nodded my head. "I'll pick you up tomorrow morning at seven."

Father met his eyes, gave a slight smile. "Yes, we'll be ready."

Herr Gruber continued. "I also own a restaurant. It's the building attached to this apartment. Frau," he nodded in the direction of Mother, "perhaps you can help me with some cleaning and cooking."

I saw Mother straighten her back, her eyes still heavy with sadness, and purse her lips into a sweet half-smile. I imagined what it would feel like, to be in the bustle of a family restaurant, so similar to what we left behind. Would it feel lovely and familiar? My heart instead felt pained, thinking of her in a kitchen without Albert and Mathias on her hip.

Mary and I laid out our bedclothes next to a thin mattress that had been placed along the wall. I don't remember falling asleep that night, only closing my eyes for a moment before waking to Father gently shaking our shoulders.

"Herr Gruber is outside. Get ready. Quickly, please." His voice was hushed, but strong. I felt strong, too. After weeks of travel and sadness, the lingering feelings of death and desperation seemed to dissipate into the promise of distraction. As the sun crested over the soft hillscape, I couldn't help but take in the freshness of the day. No rain, no freight car, just miles and miles of uninterrupted green.

Father, Joshi, Mary, and I bumped our way to the vineyard in the back of Herr Gruber's truck. When we arrived, there were three other men and four large, beautiful horses. Mary rushed out of the truck as soon as it stopped, breathless, to pet the chestnut coat of the largest one.

"What's his name?" She beamed, smiling for the first time since we left Hungary.

"*Desolee.*" The man shrugged his shoulders, curling his lip under his teeth.

"French," Herr Gruber said, hoisting empty crates out of the truck's flatbed. "They're soldiers who mainly take care of these horses for my neighbors, but also work for me during the harvest. They mostly keep to themselves."

He handed us gloves.

"Have you ever picked grapes before?"

The four of us shook our heads.

"The key is to be delicate. Cut right above the fruit." He held a bunch of grapes out from the vine and, with a quick stroke of his knife, separated them from the stem.

Herr Gruber made it seem effortless, but over the days and weeks and months that we worked for him, we learned quickly that it was much more difficult. And not only were we managing the clumsiness of holding the knife while trying not to smash the grapes, our backs ached at the end of each day from hunching over to get the fruit at the lowest part of the vine.

During our break for lunch, we'd eat mashed potatoes with a small cut of meat. In the evenings, Mother would bring back food from the restaurant—mostly potatoes, soup, and bread—and we'd tell stories about the day. At first, we were too tired to say anything. Too exhausted, too sad.

One night we came home later than usual, dinner already waiting for us at the apartment. On our way home, the skies had opened. A deluge of late autumn rain drenched us in the flatbed of the truck. My hair, flattened against my head, dripped into my eyes as I stormed into our small room, cold and wet and utterly distressed. Mary, also soaked, was quick behind me, the rain pushing her hair into her eyes. When I stopped only inches from the door, her body slammed into mine, causing me to tumble onto the ground, my body catching Mary's as she fell into me, yelling at the top of her lungs from the surprise.

My hair sticking to my ears, my blouse soaked, arguing as we untangled ourselves. I almost missed it in my frenzy. At first quiet, then louder until we couldn't help but stop and look up at our mother, laughing so hard tears were running down her face. Father and Joshi, standing in the doorway, looked just as ridiculous as Mary and I, their hairlines pressed into an uneven edge along their scalps as though they were mis-painted marionette puppets.

Mother's laughter caused a cascade of giggles and fits until all of us were holding our stomachs, gasping for air. I couldn't remember the last time we had laughed—the last time I had seen Mother smile like that. The rain had released us, if only for a moment, allowing us to feel unbridled and unburdened for the first time in months.

Chapter 14

Every week Herr Gruber would give father a bottle of wine as a thank you for our work. He'd place it in his luggage, saving it for the occasional visits from Mr. Petrović, the neighbor who had taken us to Hungary in his truck. Taking the train to visit us, he'd stay only for two glasses of wine before heading back to Betschkerck. He always came with an update for us on the Serbian bakers, telling us what was happening to the abandoned storefronts in the Jewish quarter. The Russians had arrived and rumors of what happened to other ethnically German families in smaller towns made my skin crawl. I looked around our small apartment, at my mattress stacked on top of Mary's in the corner of the room. I vowed that I'd go to sleep grateful, if only for one night, pressing out any urges for our childhood bedroom from my mind. We were alive. It was all that mattered. It was the only thing that had to matter.

As the war unraveled, so had the money. We couldn't count on our dinars to hold value for much longer. One morning, Mother woke us up earlier than usual and told us to get the coats that had our money sewed into the lining.

She took a small needle and started tearing out the seams, collecting the small bundles into a canvas bag.

"Uncle Neemer is meeting me here, in a few hours," she said, struggling with the stitches we had hurriedly placed as we were preparing to flee Betschkerck.

"Uncle Neemer?" I recognized the name, but didn't remember exactly who this relative was.

"Your grandmother's brother. He sang at the Vienna Opera before the war." She cut the thread with her teeth.

"He's going with me to an international bank nearby to help me exchange our dinars into Reichsmarks." Mother counted the bills in front of her, re-stacked them neatly, and placed them into her purse.

Uncle Neemer didn't come inside, but I heard his voice echo against the apartment's brick facade. Sweet and song-like, it was another connection to a world that felt so far away. We had only heard the harshness of strange voices, of strange languages and now, to hear the lilt of kinship float through the window…I closed my eyes and took a deep breath as though I could breathe in the familiar sound of family.

When she returned, dusk had already set in, the sky streaked with ribbons of orange and blush. Mother called me into the kitchen where she sat at the table with father.

"Else, we were able to get 30,000 Reichsmarks," Father began. I didn't know if that was a lot or too little, but I knew that money was money and would be essential for however long we were away from home.

"Like before, we need to divide it up among ourselves in case we get separated." Mother handed me a small bundle of bills. I counted them quickly.

"Ten thousand?"

"I'll also have ten thousand. So will your mother." Father stood and wrapped his arm around my shoulders. He pulled me close, squeezing me into him. "This is only a precaution, Else. We'll be okay. As long as we stay together, we'll be okay."

Chapter 15

Fall crept into the vineyard as we picked grapes and tended the vines, which turned from green to brown, the season unfolding into early winter. The snow caps on the peaks that surrounded us grew longer and heavier, blanketing the mountains in a glittering frost that burned against the pale blue sky.

By February 1945, the apartment was too small, too swollen with weary people. Our days too long, filled with uncertainty. Father decided to take a train to a large town near Kirchberg where we had heard about a displaced persons camp established in a military base that had been previously used by the Germans. He hoped that, once again, his skills as a baker would be needed and that he'd be able to find some kind of employment while we waited for the war to end.

Father left early one morning, before Herr Gruber arrived to take us to the vineyards. By the time he returned home, the sky was an inky black, the stars piercing through the blanket of night like shards of glass.

He walked through the threshold of the apartment and removed his hat. Mother stirred next to me on the thin mattress that we pulled into the middle of the room each night. As she stood up, I could feel her looking at me, checking to see if I was still asleep. I had woken up, but kept my eyes closed and my body still.

The floor creaked as she started walking toward the door to greet him; I imagined her outstretching her arms to pull him into a long embrace—the kind they reserved for moments away from their children.

Their conversation was hushed, sputtering out in brief bursts of whisper.

"They offered me…"

"...could smell the sickness…"

"But it's housing, yes? And food?"

"....will there be other…."

"...I keep hearing that the Germans…."

I tried to knit together the fragments of conversation I could hear, but soon I was waking to Mary shaking me.

"Else, you overslept. Herr Gruber will be here with the truck in mere moments!" she squeaked, throwing my work clothes onto my pile of blankets.

I looked at Father as we rode to the vineyards. His face betrayed nothing of the news he brought home with him last night. I wanted to ask if we'd be moving, if he found a job, if we'd finally get an apartment with space enough to stretch our legs when we slept.

Father held off until we finished our workday and arrived back to the room above the restaurant. Held off until Mother finished working, my eyes already heavy from a long day of bailing wire from the unused vineyard patches as the cold bit my fingers. We huddled together on the floor, Frankie in the middle, fast asleep with his head in my lap.

"I got a job," Father began. "There's a displaced persons camp not too far from here, still in Austria. And they need a baker."

My heart leapt.

There was no pay, but they'd provide food and housing. I looked around the room, our neat piles of clothes and bedding and meager stockpile of food merging into the brown/gray mass and decided, sight unseen, that it would be better than what we had.

It was bleaker than I could have imagined. The camp was for displaced persons who had no money and for the very ill with communicable diseases. Diphtheria and typhus were rampant, and in an attempt to control further outbreaks, no one could leave the camp without a compelling reason.

I found a job at the main office issuing permits that allowed individuals to leave the premises for day-long periods of time. How does one examine a situation to determine another's eligibility for freedom? We continued to be judge and juror of humanity—the soldiers in Betschkerck throwing Jews into wagons, the Austrians picking over German refugees for work, and now here, at the displaced persons camp, assessing what necessitated undeniable exemption from reality.

We had little money, and still, no country. But being employed by the camp separated us from the others and protected us from disease. The German soldiers had been managing the camp when we arrived at the end of February, but as the weeks ticked by, they began to leave—first in small teams of three or four relocated to a different part of the front, then suddenly, by April, all at once.

The gentle breeze of spring mixed with the tension of our uncertain future. The camp seemed to tremble with a sense of looming chaos. When Joshi, now twelve, became very ill, Mother knew he had to go to the hospital within the confines of camp, but hesitated until his throat bloomed red, too swollen to swallow solid food.

It was mid-April and we could feel the war shift, its end imminent. The Germans were losing. They had lost. The snippets of news we received didn't give us many details, but the sudden absence of soldiers unsettled any brief moment of respite we had found.

It happened slowly, then all at once: a few trepid individuals taking an extra loaf of bread; a young teenager carefully, hesitantly, opening the administrative building's front door before walking out with a pile of fresh blankets. Soon the camp, absent of order, descended into chaos as cabinets and shelves were pillaged and order was upended. Mother, noticing the shift, knew that the only thing more dangerous than the illusion of safety was the blatant disregard for structure.

Father had already left for the bakery when I walked into the kitchen and saw Mother sitting at the table. Another quiet morning, her brow furrowed as she made notes in a small notebook in front of her. This again, I thought, wondering what would happen next.

"Else," she kept writing. "This is too much." She paused, looking up at me. In the months that had followed our first flight from Betschkerck, I had become her confidante while Father was away at work.

"I don't feel good about our family staying here." Her lips pressed into a thin line. "It doesn't feel safe, with Germany losing the war, to be with other displaced Germans..." She trailed off. I knew she was thinking about what had happened to Father's family when the Russians invaded Yugoslavia. She stood.

"I'm going to get your brother from the hospital and then we're going to leave."

My mouth gaped in confusion. As I pulled my eyebrows together, Mother seemed to read my mind.

"I don't know where we're going next. We'll head to the train station first. Your father left early this morning to let the bakery know that we're leaving." She pulled her coat off of the small peg next to the apartment door, pulling her arms through the sleeves in short, hurried bursts. "I need you to pack with Mary and Frankie while I get Joshi."

It took us only an hour to gather our belongings, which had been reduced to a small collection of food and clothing, our Reichsmarks sewn into the lining of winter coats.

It took Mother a long time to return with Joshi. When they walked through the door he was pale and listless. I could tell the walk from the hospital had been taxing. Mother brushed his hair from his forehead, glistened with a fevered sweat.

Outside, the stench of sickness and feces had thickened. The air was thick with body odor and trash everywhere. We saw Father approaching the apartment, a small bag of burnt bread in his hands, which he gave to Mary.

He lowered into a crouch before Joshi.

"Do you think you're strong enough to hold your arms around my neck if I carry you on my back?"

Joshi nodded weakly.

Chapter 16

The nearest train station was only a few kilometers away and by the time we arrived the platform was trembling with crowds of families trying to find a seat on any train, going anywhere.

We entered into the crush of bodies, the air filled with shouting, with the exhalation of steam from the train engine. The mass of people pressed into any train that pulled into the station. I held tightly onto Mary's hand.

"Else! Mary! Frankie!" I heard Father's voice stretch across the noise and looked up to find him. We locked eyes and he tilted his head toward the street, away from the trains. We pushed through, following him until we felt a sharp release from the throng.

I heard an exhaust pipe choke loudly and turned to see Mother handing carefully counted bills to a German soldier standing next to a large army truck. We followed her around back and pulled ourselves up onto the flatbed. The truck lurched forward as we fell onto the floor packed with boxes and bags, supplies that they were evacuating from the surrounding area.

"I paid them 500 Marks to take us back to Gruber's vineyard," Mother whispered loudly. We were too tired, too overwhelmed to respond, but she continued, as if to answer the question she had expected.

"It's just to figure out what's next. I'll see if they'll let me work at the restaurant for a bit while we determine where we're going."

We had only just settled into the small familiar room when we heard from Henry. We were entering our second week at the vineyard, again hunched over vines (this time pruning dead wood), again eating green potatoes and leftover scrap meat. It had become difficult to anticipate how long we'd stay in one place, if we'd need to move quickly. Whenever we received a letter from our brother, it always felt like a bit of magic: unexplained and bewildering.

My dear family,

I hope this letter reaches you in time. We've heard that the Russians will be moving into Austria as the army retreats. I'm being released from service and will try to make it to Bavaria. If you can make it there as well, I'll find you. Don't hesitate. Leave immediately.
Henry

We stood in a circle, Father dangling the letter, newly read, from his fingertips as we looked at each other in silence.

"Well." Mary hesitated softly and caught her breath. "I've always wanted to visit Bavaria."

Her words lingered in the air, their lightness cutting across the heaviness of the news that Henry had sent. We smiled at each other, not exuberantly—we were far from laughter as a soft, resigned sadness settled in—but we smiled nonetheless. Quietly, we turned to our belongings, packing them again in what felt like an agreed-upon silence. I brushed a tear away with the back of my hand as Mother left the room to once again determine how we'd leave.

Chapter 17

I held Mary's hand, squeezing tightly as the truck hit another shallow ditch in the road, sending our heads into the truck's ceiling. Even though it was April, Father's coat was buttoned up to his chin, his hands stuffed into his pockets. I nestled into Mary, trying to stay warm.

Mother had found a German officer who was willing to help us make travel arrangements to Bavaria for a small fee, but when we arrived at the meeting point, the truck was already halfway full.

The officer shrugged his shoulders, his mouth fixed into a firm line. My mother demanded an explanation—clenched her fists at her side and argued that the money she gave him guaranteed passage for all six of us. He listened and, when she stopped speaking, calmly told her there was only room for three. But, if we wanted, there was another, much larger, cargo truck that was leaving shortly, and whoever didn't fit on this truck could leave with the other convoy. Mother boarded the first truck going to Bavaria with Joshi and Frankie because they were younger.

Older, and better equipped to manage the uncertainty of the journey, it was decided that Mary and I would join Father in the second truck. Already standing on the truck's flatbed, Father pulled up our bags to use as makeshift seats. The waxed canvas cover kept us dry, but the wind began to bite, a lingering remnant of winter. We didn't know where we were going, only that we were going west, toward Germany, shoulder to shoulder with nearly twenty other people. Our companions were mostly young soldiers and a few civilians, like us, who were trying to evade the Russians.

As darkness descended, Mary and I pressed the sides of our heads together in an attempt to sleep. By morning, my chin had dropped against my clavicle, my neck stretched beyond feeling. I wiped the sleep from my eyes.

Mary groaned. Her head had fallen back and was now lopsided, her ear grazing her left shoulder.

"Why aren't we moving?" Her eyes were still closed.

My discomfort had distracted me from noticing that the truck was still. And that Father, and half of our traveling companions, were gone. I stood up. Even though it was still cold, the early morning light had already transitioned into its warm, spring hue. A barn swallow called out in the distance. Jumping out of the flatbed, I could hear an officer barking at a soldier a few meters away from the truck, as a larger group of soldiers stood around its open hood, obscured in steam. It took me only a few seconds to make out my father's silhouette: a baker among the young lieutenants.

"The truck broke down earlier this morning, Else," he whispered through the side of his mouth. "They can't seem to figure out how to get it up and running."

I looked around. We stood on a dirt road flanked by fields that stretched as far as I could see, yellow rapeseed flowers sprouting blossoms. The barn swallow continued to sing.

"Where are we?" I asked. He pressed his lips together and shook his head while he shrugged his shoulders.

"I'm going to check on Mary." I squeezed his hand and walked to the back of the truck.

I found her rubbing her eyes, light streaming through the openings in the canvas cover, illuminating soft specks of dirt and dust.

"Where are we?" she asked, blowing her nose and standing.

"The truck broke down," I began to reply as a banging sounded on the side of the truck.

"Anyone else still inside, please come out," a voice barked.

We jumped out, walking over to Father, who was talking with some of the other passengers. He pointed into the field, at two soldiers walking toward a small farmhouse, the only dwelling for miles, perched at the top of a shallow hill that crested gently over the crops. The early morning dusk hung heavy, the air still hushed with lingering darkness.

"They're going to see if they'll let us stay at the house until the truck can be fixed."

The spring light had warmed, but the air was still cold. We exhaled thin clouds of breath as we watched the soldiers approach the door and knock. They knocked again. We saw them reach for their belts, taking out flashlights, shining the light into the windows. There was shouting, more knocking, more thumping until we saw the door crack and then, a small woman, arms crossed and angry, in its threshold.

It took most of the day to unload the truck. We had brought a few parcels of food, but nothing that could last much past the afternoon. I had assumed that we'd arrive somewhere that would have food—a displaced persons camp, perhaps. Or a military base. As I thumbed the last piece of bread in my pocket, I realized I didn't know what I was expecting next. That my mother and brothers were far from us, that I was now sitting in an open field in the middle of nowhere.

Would we ever go back home? Would I see Sera and Anica? Would we run to the lake, gossiping about the boys who were trying to grow mustaches, their upper lips patchy and unformed? I thought of those boys, so young, so desperate to be old. I wondered if they had found themselves at the front, like my brother Henry; if they were still alive. Were they also in fields, banging on doors of unsuspecting old ladies? Had their soft sweetness evaporated?

That night we crowded into the kitchen, unrolled the few blankets that we had, and tried to get some sleep. I pressed myself against the wall, with Mary behind me and father behind her. The soldiers, used to sleeping anywhere, fell quickly into slumber. We tried to sleep through the rumble of rolling snores and cold drafts of wind that crept into the kitchen, our coats wrapped tightly around us.

I barely slept. As the morning light streamed through the windows, I felt my stomach pinch announcing a pang of sharp hunger; my mouth felt dry. The day before, a few other soldiers had found nearby farms with scrap potatoes to spare. They were ugly, misshapen, with black spots, beginning to sprout. But it was food that we desperately needed.

I lifted myself off the floor, left the house, and went around back to find the well. I filled a small bucket with water and tried to arrange it over the pile of cold coals from the night before. The owner of the house hadn't allowed us inside until nightfall, relegating us to the kitchen (only the kitchen) for shelter, making it clear that we couldn't touch anything. One of the younger soldiers was already up, a nice boy with an impish smile. He made me feel more comfortable than the others and walked over to help me re-start the coals.

The water boiled and cooked the potatoes until we could bite into them without much trouble, but not enough to make them soft and creamy. I was so hungry that I barely noticed the potato starch coating the insides of my mouth and stomached its rancid sourness. As I sat by the fire, my throat swelled and my eyes stung. The noise of the birds, of the wind, of the early morning conversation melded into a wall of gray static. My hands trembled. Beyond the house I saw a thicket of trees and, without thinking, ran.

The world melted into nothing, the field transformed into the moss-laden forest floor. My stomach lurched up bits of moldy potato. I fell to the ground, at the base of an old evergreen tree, and let the tears stream down my face, tasting the salt of so many days and nights without comfort or rest. Why would I go back? To the farmhouse, to Betschkerck, to Yugoslavia?

No, I decided, my mind still enveloped in the fog of fatigue and despair, I would stay here. I would live here, in the forest near the small farmhouse, near the field where the old truck broke down. The canopy of fir trees would protect me and I would disappear into their deep green needles.

"Else!"

I pushed it away, the sound of my voice being called, as it threatened to pull me back to the farmhouse, to the truck.

"Else!"

I clapped my hands over my ears and closed my eyes tightly.

"Else!"

Even before the war (and in spite of it), Mary's voice had a scintillating lilt that bubbled over when she was excited or frustrated or scared. When we were younger, it had made it hard to take her seriously; when we were in a truck finding our way to the German border, it had made the journey easier to manage. Comforting, even. And now, as I heard her yell my name, over and over and over again, it pulled me back to where I was: alone, in the woods, near an old farmhouse where my father and sister waited for me to return.

But did I want to return? Mary held my elbow softly, her hand on my back, and guided me back to the small pit fire, back to the potatoes and the soldiers. We sat quietly, staring into the hot coals.

"I'm so tired," I whispered, a tear falling down my cheek. Mary placed her head on my shoulder.

◆◆◆◆

I heard Frankie giggle before I heard her voice. The endless stream of mishaps and confusion had made any kind of hope for miracles scarce, but there she was. My mother, beautiful and resilient.

She was talking to Father when we ran up to her. I fell into her embrace, my full weight in her arms, my face buried in her scarf. She said nothing, stroking my hair with her hand as I wept.

Before Mother had boarded the truck with Frankie and Joshi, the driver had assured her that both trucks would follow the same road. She made him promise, looking over her shoulder to see us waiting for our truck to arrive. "We have already come this far," I imagined her telling the driver, her eyes firm. When the truck didn't show up for hours, I knew she pinned him to the wall with her stare, asking him to explain, then telling him to take them back along the road to find her family. The driver made her pay him a small fee, but she wouldn't risk our separation. Not now.

"You were much closer than I anticipated," she said, smiling, as I laid my head in her lap. "We retraced the road until we saw the broken-down truck. After that, it was easy enough to find the farmhouse."

Mother stroked my hair as a breeze came across the front porch of the farmhouse, where we sat, our backs pressed together, propping each other up, as we'd grown accustomed.

She began to hum a quiet tune, one I recognized from my childhood, slow and melodic. Mary joined in, their voices woven together, almost dancing with the wind.

As I closed my eyes, the forest disappeared and I fell asleep for what felt like days.

That evening, the six of us sat on the front porch of the farmhouse, eating sandwiches Mother had made before she had left with the boys. I watched dusk fall across the field, the yellow flowers blushing in the glow of a setting sun.

They moved us into the barn, next to the house. It smelled like cow shit, filled with flies that bred in piles of dung that dotted the floor. We piled stale hay into a corner of one of the stalls and covered what we could with a blanket that Mother kept in her suitcase. That night the rats clicked their teeth as we slept.

"Tsst tsst tsst!" my father hissed. I heard a thud; a rodent yelped.

In the morning, Father was slumped against the stall's wall, snoring. Mother was next to him, her arms wrapped around a large board.

Her eyes flickered open and held mine.

"We kept the rats away, Else." She smiled, before closing her eyes. "We kept them all away."

It was a week before the soldiers were able to find local mechanics to repair the truck. We left the farmhouse, the barn, the rats, the moss-laden forest and continued on. Through fields and hills, we made our way toward Germany, into Bavaria, to a small town called Freilassing, just over the Austrian border.

The train engine steam flooded the station as we unloaded ourselves from the truck. There was a displaced persons camp in Niedernfels, Germany, closer to the French border and, as we gave our names to the Red Cross volunteers, I heard a barn swallow call in the distance as a warbler flew across the horizon.

Else: April 28, 1945

The night is still. My mother stands next to me on the platform of the train station in Freilassing, the air cool and peaceful. Finally, peaceful. Our family is as whole as it can be, and safe. Soon we'll see Henry and then we'll be together. I push Mathias out of my head, if only for a moment. There is no room for sadness, at least not now. Only hope, a thread of relief that we'll use to pull ourselves into quiet serenity. I don't know where we'll go after Niedernfels, but we won't have to run anymore. The war will end, we'll be far from the Russians. Father will bake bread. Henry and I will play our accordions. Joshi will teach Frankie how to pull pranks and he'll shift back into his mischievous boyhood.

Absent-mindedly I rub my hands together and think of Henry. I wonder what it will be like to see him again after all this time—will he look more grown? Will we recognize him?

It's quiet as we stand, waiting for the train that will take us to the displaced persons camp in Niedernfels, but I feel the stillness shift and hang. It lingers, suspended, until the night suddenly erupts.

There's light and noise, sulfur and smoke, the ground lifting up beneath us as we run. The planes are low, ripping through the night. We hear the explosions before we feel the dirt kick up.

The taste of metal floods my mouth as I'm thrown to the ground, the stone scraping my cheek. I try to push myself back up, but my body is forced back into the pavement as the air presses us down with the sound of hollow popping, short explosions that echo in my head.

I push my knees into my chest, pull my body upright, and run. Mother is in front of me with Frankie, their bodies a blur. The only instinct I have, primal and wild, is to follow my mother, to hold onto the sight of her red scarf as my legs move as fast as I can manage. I feel Mary peel away from my side. I turn my head back to see Father crouched behind our belongings. There is no sound, but I see his mouth moving. His hands wave me forward; push me toward Mother.

The earth lurches violently; the sky screams as we run.

I follow Mother into a small yard behind a stone building and watch her throw her body over Frankie. I crumple beside her, my hands clasped over the back of my neck. With each explosion, my body tightens until I cannot feel where my legs end and the ground begins. My eyelids press together until the world is white, blinding. Empty.

And then, as quickly as the sky lit up with fire, there is silence. The darkness is deafening.

I unwind my body and see Mother pulling herself off Frankie, groaning as she settles onto her back. There is blood. It bubbles slowly out of her lower leg, thick and viscous.

"Mother!" I scream. Or, I think I scream. My ears burn.

She grasps her leg. Her mouth moves silently (or is she also screaming?) The buzzing in my ears gets louder, sharper. I watch her put her weight on her elbows, her body shuttering as she tries to stand.

I pull off my belt and hold it around her thigh, pulling tightly, but the blood keeps streaming out of a wound the size of my forearm, a piece of shrapnel lodged between muscle and bone.

I look for Mary and Joshi and find them in a ditch not far beyond from where we were standing. The ground feels like it is on fire, smoke rising from piles of dirt and debris, clouds of dust kicked up like a thick fog. I see them crawling out of the earth, patches of hair missing from their heads, a thin layer of blood on Mary's face. Our bodies collide as we run toward each other, my hands frantically searching their heads, their necks, their torsos for wounds, for blood. I find nothing. The air shifts and moves as cries get louder around us. Sirens are screaming. My lungs feel like they're filled with petrol and charcoal, sulfur, and smoke.

I cry for Father, cry for help, run as I cry, trying not to trip over rubble that's crumbled in the middle of the street. I run as fast as my legs will let me, and then press them to go faster, still. I hear tires crunching, hear them move slowly into the wreckage, people shouting for help, for assistance, lifting injured bodies up and out of the chaos, into small wagons.

I continue to scream for Father, can only hear my blood rushing into my brain, feel the pressure of my heartbeat in my temples. My legs move as quickly as I can manage.

I find him still on the train platform, the station in piles around him. He is sitting on our luggage, dazed and bloody. I run to him, falling in front of his feet.

"I flew, Else…" his voice trails off, weak. "…I fell and was hit by something…" He leans his body against his arm, which rests on top of the suitcase.

A small bell dings and I see a man dressed in dirty trousers, a floppy cap, navigating his bicycle toward us. He motions for me to bring Father to him.

"Can he walk? Put him on my bike. I'll take him to the hospital," he motions away from the train station. "Only five minutes from here."

I help Father up, slowly. On his feet, he vomits blood. His body goes slack as I lift him up by his armpits. The man wheels his bicycle in front of him. Father places his hand on the seat and gets sick again.

"He's too weak," I say as I lower him to the ground. But there is a child's wagon, down the street, next to what was the wall of a house, now a pile of stones. Its red lacquer finish bursts through the mounds of rusted metal and gray rock.

The man helps me put Father into the wagon, his body folded into the shallow bin. Handle in hand, I run again. The heat from the explosions makes me perspire, sweat falling into my eyes, the night growing darker as we move further from the station. My stomach sours from the smell of iron and fire; bile rises into my mouth as my stomach heaves.

One foot in front of the other, I pull the wagon over gravel, over dirt, over branches that fall into our path. I feel my legs moving quickly but it feels as though we're not making any progress, as though I'm walking through mud, through a wall of shouting and screaming.

But there is a tent. A white flag with a red cross. The hurried motions of uniformed men and women who scoop Father out of the wagon, onto a stretcher and whisk him under the tent where beds have been lined along the perimeter. I follow until I see Mother, in a bed, sheets soaked with blood. She is here, but she is also not here, her eyes flickering shut, her body drenched in rusted red.

"Lissie!" I hear Father's hoarse screaming as he redirects the medics carrying his stretcher to her bed. His arm extends toward her, so much so that his torso nearly falls out of the stretcher.

"Tetanus…tetanus….tetanus…." She is whimpering the same thing over and over until a nurse arrives with a syringe.

"She demanded a tetanus shot as soon as she arrived," the nurse tells me as she administers the vaccine. I think of Mathias, then push the image of his stiff body out of my mind as quickly as it arrives.

Father is lowered into a chair next to her. He holds her hand in his as I crumpled to the floor, into the safety of the unlit corner. In the quiet cocoon of darkness, my head falls into my knees and I cry.

Chapter 18

As the sun began to rise, Mary, Joshi, Frankie, and I crumpled into a pile on the steps of the hospital. Even though oranges and pinks streaked across the sky as the darkness melted into a pale blue and the long night ended, we felt the serenity of sleep sweep into our bodies.

It was short-lived. We woke only hours later, at first forgetting what we had survived, then gripped with the recollection of reality. My body stiffened as I remembered our parents, injured and bleeding. We were hungry. And thirsty. Our bags, which once numbered nearly forty, were down to fifteen, and we had nothing to eat or drink. When we saw the truck arrive to take those of us who had survived the bombing to the camp where we had hoped to meet up with Henry, I knew I had to decide what we would do: stay here and wait for our parents to heal, with no food or provisions, or to leave them with a thread of hope for a reunion in a few weeks.

I entered the hospital. The sour, metallic stench of blood made my stomach turn. In the corner I saw Father slumped over in a chair next to Mother's bed, her face pale and listless. Her eyes fluttered as I approached the bed.

"They want to take us to Niedernfels," I told them, my voice, quiet so as to not disturb the other patients who moaned and fought with sleep.

Father looked at me, his eyes weak and tired. "Go, Else," he said. Mother groaned, as if in agreement. "You can't stay here. Henry is waiting for us." He closed his eyes, his body pinched with pain. I nodded without protest.

My eyes welled with tears as I leaned forward to kiss his forehead. I knelt next to Mother, her body beaded with sweat. "I love you, Mama," I breathed into her ear, resorting to a name I hadn't called her since I was a young child.

Outside the hospital, in the midday sun, I saw my sister and brothers waiting expectantly. I don't know what they thought I'd tell them. That, perhaps, we'd stay or that we'd convince the soldiers to transport our parents with us to the camp. But this is what I had learned the moment I saw blood seep out of my mother's leg: that we were no longer children and we had to learn how to move forward without our parents. The innocence of childhood, what had remained after we fled Yugoslavia, had evaporated as bombs exploded and bullets descended.

For a moment I could smell the chalk, as I sat in my first Catechism class in Tschetereg. Could feel my hair braided down my back, and my white stockings slide down to my ankles. I could see the nun's white wimple pressing into the side of her plump face as she recited the Ten Commandments, instructing us to repeat after her, while above her desk a verse in stern calligraphy:

"When I was a child, I spoke as a child, I understood as a child,
I thought as a child: but when I became a man,
I put away childish things."

On the steps of a hospital in Freilassing, as my mother lay in blood-soaked sheets, I let go of the remaining scraps of childhood that I had held onto. I straightened my back, swallowed the lump in my throat, and descended into the arms of Mary. I held her as tightly as she had held me before pulling away to wrap Joshi and Frankie into our embrace.

"We're going to continue on to Niedernfels," I began. "Which means we need to leave Mother and Father behind."

No one said anything. Mary wiped a tear from her cheek with the back of her hand. Quietly we loaded our remaining luggage into the truck.

As we drove toward the camp, I turned my body so I could see the hospital. As the exhaust pipe sputtered, I etched their faces into my memory and the truck picked up speed. When I could no longer see the hospital, when the building disappeared behind a thicket of trees, I faced forward to look, unwaveringly, down the gravel road.

Lissie: Freilassing Hospital, April 1945

I continue to bleed, the bed linens now a dark rusted red. Twice a day the nurses change my bandages, which are soaked through, deteriorating until they're nearly unrecognizable. My mind feels disconnected from my body, a body which feels both flimsy and dense. I see spots of light flicker in and out of my gaze; hear Mathias babble. He calls me Mama over and over again, even though I can't seem to figure out where he is. And there is darkness, then a bright light, then darkness again.

I feel a calloused hand caress my own. I breathe Jen's but the voice isn't his. No, it's lower, softer and Per istam sanctan unctionem and misericordiam *and* holy child *and my eyes flicker open and see a clerical collar soaked in sweat. I push Mathias's sweet voice away. I push it away and I tell him I'm sorry but I can't hear his voice anymore because if I do, if he stays, I'll leave and I can't. I can't just yet, I tell him and try to remember his blue eyes and tell him I love him and I push him away until all I can see is the priest and his collar which is no longer white but yellowed like decaying flesh and when I hold my hand out, he goes to grab it, tenderly, but I know that if he takes my hand he'll keep talking and I don't want him to talk anymore. I grab his sleeve and his eyes grow wide and I hold on tightly because I've already pushed Mathias away because Else and Mary and Joshi and Henry and Frankie and there is no time for last rites because I pushed Mathias away and there is too much left.*

My sheets are red and my bandages are red and my body still threatens to leave, but I tell the priest that I'm not dying and with his mouth still agape he seems to flutter and disappears and returns with a doctor.

I am on a stretcher in a truck that rattles, that makes my teeth clash loudly in my mouth and I wish for Jens but he is not here, he is sick too they tell me, too sick to rattle next to me and we rattle and stop and rattle and stop, each time they tell me this will be the last stop but each time we keep moving until there is a man who looks at me and tells me his name is Dr. Mueller and that he'll take care of me, but by now there is more darkness than light and I can barely make out his face, can only hear him tell the nurse she only has a ten percent chance, but we'll try and then it is dark again. I search for Mathias's voice, but it is gone. And then it is as bright and as brilliant as the morning sun.

Chapter 19

This is what Mother would later tell us. That after she refused her last rites, after Dr. Mueller saved her life. That after the bleeding stopped and her leg was set and casted, she knew we'd be together again. There was a Polish man, she'd tell us, who came to visit his girlfriend who was in the same hospital ward as Mother in Fridolfing, a small Bavarian town 25 kilometers north of Freilassing.

"His smile was so sweet," she told us. "He'd always bring her flowers from the meadow outside our window."

◆ ◆ ◆ ◆

The Germans surrendered in May. Mary, Joshi, Frankie, and I were in Niedernfels, at the displaced persons camp, attempting to move forward without our parents, unsure where Henry was. There was celebration throughout the camp, but it couldn't penetrate my sadness. The familiar bellows of the accordion, the singing, the shouts of laughter reminded me only of our family and what we had lost. The war was over, but in so many ways, our lives had just begun—or rather, were waiting to start again as we sat in the liminality of the unknown. This was not home, but home was no longer home. I tried to imagine what home would become, but without Mother or Father or Henry, it was impossible. Instead, I felt so very alone.

When first we arrived at the camp, they shuffled us into an empty school, into one of its classrooms that we shared with three other families. In our bags, we had only a loaf of bread; my stomach churned with hunger.

One of the women approached me as Mary began to organize a small corner of the room that we decided to claim. She wore a faded blue kerchief in her hair, pants, and a men's shirt with its sleeves rolled up to her elbows.

"Where are you coming from?" she asked me in accented German.

"Betschkerck," I began, before stuttering out, "Uh, Yugoslavia," when I saw her eyebrows knit together in confusion.

"Ah!" She wiped her forehead with her hand, the midday humidity rising. "Me? I'm from Poland. Is it just the four of you? No parents?"

My face winced, inadvertently betraying my anxiety. She quickly shifted past her question.

"No matter. You need food, yes? After the nurse inspects you for lice, you'll go to city hall in town and get ration tickets for what you need."

She threaded her arm through my elbow.

"The lines are usually long, but it's not so bad once you figure out a system." She pulled me close, then released my arm. As she walked toward the door, she turned back to the room, adding, "I'll let you know where I get meat."

We were instructed to go to the nurse's office first. One by one, she inspected us for lice, pulling the hairs on my head apart with little regard to comfort or gentleness. I knew we didn't have lice, but even as we unbuttoned, unzipped, unlaced our clothes and shoes and braced ourselves for the cold decontamination shower, I knew that we were in no position to argue against protocol.

My shoes, wet with decontamination spray, squelched as I walked back to the classroom.

"I hate this," I thought bitterly, holding wet clothes that had also been sprayed while we were in the delousing shower. I wore a light muslin shift dress with rough fabric that made my skin itch. The nurse had handed it to me, her mouth in a tight line, and told me to make sure we cleaned ourselves regularly.

"Of course," was all I could manage. Stay clean? Of course. Find food? Of course. Leave home at a moment's notice? Of course. Mary came alongside me, her fingers laced with mine.

"What if I try to find some flowers for the classroom, hmmm?" She hummed as she walked. I couldn't help but smile, feeling the day's burden release. Try to find some beauty? Of course.

On Mondays I walked into town to get our ration tickets from city hall, just like Olga, our Polish roommate, had told me. I then stood in line at the baker and the grocer, some days for hours on end. On Saturday, I'd go to another town with Olga to stand in line at the butcher's.

"Better quality here," she told me the first morning I went with her as I watched lines weave out of small shops and snake their way into alleys and cobblestone streets.

During the rest of the week I washed our clothes, wrote letters that I hoped to send to Mother and Father once we determined where they were. I didn't know if they had stayed in Freilassing or if they were transported elsewhere. I wondered if Mother was still alive, then pushed the thought from my head. At night, I took our small accordion, only slightly damaged from the bombing, and played at the dance hall.

American soldiers came to dance with their girlfriends most nights. "It's because we're not German," Olga told me one Saturday morning, as we stood in the meat line. They were sweet, but most only spoke English and kept to themselves.

"Hey! Your name?" I looked up, surprised. One of the young American soldiers was looking at me. He repeated his question, again in clumsy, stilted Serbian. "Your name?"

"Else," I said quietly. Mary saw who I was talking to and walked over as though she had springs in her shoes.

"I'm Mary!" she extended her hand out confidently and shook his. "What's yours?"

Tony was from Topeka, Kansas. "Very flat," he said, rolling his eyes. He was friends with Will, another American soldier, who spoke German better than Tony spoke Serbian.

"Your family is here?" Will asked.

"Well, kind of," Mary began. "There's me and Else, but also our brothers Joshi and Frankie." She motioned toward the schoolhouse where they were sleeping.

"Mom and Dad?" Tony asked in German. Will punched him in the arm. It may have been taboo to inquire about unmentioned family members, but we didn't mind.

"No really it's okay," I said. "We don't know where they are. They were hurt in a bombing last month and had to stay behind with the Red Cross while we continued to Niedernfels." These were the facts and this was how I kept my mind focused. If I strayed too far away from what I knew and indulged in the "what ifs," I'd go mad. Repeating the facts to strangers, to Tony and Will, made them solidify, made them even more real: we were there, now we're here and they are somewhere else. The facts kept the door propped open for hope.

"Oh man." Tony sighed into his beer and took a big gulp. He set down his glass, wiped his mouth with his hand, and looked at us with wide, melancholy eyes. "So you don't know where they are? Or if they're still hurt?"

Mary and I looked at each other then shook our heads.

Tony ran his fingers through his hair. "I'm so sorry," he said. I could tell he wanted to say more but we had reached the limit of language—we couldn't understand English, his Serbian vocabulary had been exhausted.

A week later, as I began my morning walk to city hall, Tony ran toward me. It was June and even the early morning was hot; his uniform was already soaked in sweat. He was out of breath but smiling.

"Your—your card!" He made a small rectangle shape with his hands, pointing to the bag on my shoulder.

"My identification card?" I said, pulling out my government-issued ID. He nodded emphatically, his grin getting wider.

"Town hall, err, travel permit." He stumbled through his Serbian, making gestures. "For your parents!"

Eventually, I pieced together what he was telling me: he could help me get a travel permit to try and find our parents. Will found us as Tony was trying to explain everything and translated in German that Tony had offered to, not only get the permit, but to take me back to Freilassing to see if we could gather any information about their whereabouts.

I didn't know what to say, so I agreed and gave him my identification card. My stomach churned in excitement and fear. The opportunity to find Father and Mother was too precious to turn down. But I didn't know Tony. Even with his kindness, there were whispers and gossip, stories of soldiers and young women that crept into my mind.

"See if Peter and Joseph can go with you," Mary suggested when I told her about Tony's offer and my nerves. Peter and Joseph, two Serbian boys who lived with their families in the classroom next door, were sweet with a boyish sense of duty. Even though they could have only been twelve, if I asked them to come with me, I knew they'd consider themselves my protectors.

With their mother's permission, a few days later, they joined me as we walked to the edge of camp to the entrance where Tony said he'd be waiting for us. Their faces serious, their steps firm, I knew that they were ready to be wary of Tony—already on guard and cautious.

As we turned the corner through the camp's gate, I heard them erupt in cheers. They pumped their fists as they ran to the shiny American Jeep with Tony behind the wheel. He jumped down, lifting the boys up into the vehicle by their armpits as they frantically touched the leather seats and metal hood.

"Else! Can you believe this?" Peter asked me, a grin bursting through his face. I smiled, shaking my head as we started down the road, toward the Autobahn. Once, a bustling thoroughfare that connected cities and people, now an empty asphalt path that melted into the distance.

Tony started driving. "Freilassing," he told me as we barreled down the abandoned road. It made sense to start where I knew we had been—where perhaps they'd still be. When I saw the hospital, I also saw my mother's blood-stained sheets, my father weeping at her bedside, the past merging with reality. What would I see after I ascended the small steps and entered the building?

I saw my father, sitting in the chair where I'd left him, his face peaceful, reading a newspaper. My heart stopped. It was as though we had simply left to get bread minutes before and were now returning to check in on him.

He looked up and gasped. Clutching his heart, he whispered, "Else?" his voice thick with emotion. I rushed to him, falling to my knees next to his chair, burying my face in his lap.

His legs were still badly injured and he was unable to walk. But his eyes shone as we talked. "I didn't know if you, if the others, were still alive." He held my face in his hands.

"We are!" I said laughing with happiness. "We're in Niedernfels, at the displaced persons camp." I put my hand over his. "I'm watching out for Mary, Joshi, and Frankie. Making sure the boys don't get into too much trouble. That we have enough food to eat. I'm even playing my accordion some nights at the dance hall," I said smiling.

"And who's this?" He tilted his head in the direction of Tony.

"He's an American soldier who comes to the camp to dance with his girlfriend. Mary and I told him about the bombing and he wanted to help us find you." I saw my father's face straighten into a stern line. "No, I don't think it's like that." I pointed to Peter and Joseph, who were standing silently next to Tony, trying hard to look intimidating enough to be my chaperones, trying even harder not to giggle. "But that's why I brought these two boys with me. They're Serbian. Very sweet." A nurse walked in front of the boys, gently helping a man with an eye patch walk down the hallway. His dressing gown, loose and unfitted, blew up with a gust of wind. Peter's eyes grew big as he hit Joseph in the arm, whispering in his ear as they descended into a fit of laughter.

Father's face softened as it broke into a smirk. "Ah yes, the best of the best."

Father told us that Mother had been taken to another hospital in a small town called Fridolfing. I felt my body relax—this meant there was a good chance that she was still alive as well. Peter excitedly interjected when he heard us talking. "Fridolfing? I know that place! I can show Tony how to get there." I looked at Father. We had only just been reunited. I wanted to stay with him, to make sure he was comfortable, that he was getting enough sleep, enough food.

He squeezed my hand gently. "Go, Else. It'll be good for her to see you."

"Are you—" I hesitated.

"I'm sure." I could tell by the pained smile that he wanted nothing more than for me to stay. To tell him about Mary's fiery spirit at the camp, or how Joshi was trying his very hardest to behave—but couldn't help but to tie my shoelaces together as a practical joke. And how I'd scold him, but find relief in the silliness amid the ever imposing daily seriousness.

"Go," he whispered, patting my leg. I told him I'd return as soon as I could. Knowing he was still in Freilassing made it easier to say goodbye.

Chapter 20

It took us less than an hour to get to Fridolfing. Peter, who couldn't speak English, leaned over the gearshift, pointing out the directions to Tony, who barely understood Serbian. As we neared the outskirts of town and headed toward the city center, I saw a young man walking alone.

"Excuse me," I shouted, still trying to sound polite. "Do you know where the hospital is?"

He turned, his eyes lighting up at the sight of an American Jeep. "I do!" he replied enthusiastically. Before we could respond, he had climbed into the back of the cab, running his hands over its shiny green enamel paint.

"Oh, yes, sorry," he looked up, smiling. "Go straight ahead, then turn left. I can direct you from there."

I felt the pressure rise in my chest, as though my heart would explode from this strange chemistry of anxiety and excitement. Would Mother be in good spirits? Would she be deformed, or unconscious, or worse, would her mental faculties be compromised? In Neidernfels, there were men and women who stayed to themselves, their eyes glassy, their mouths taut. The first time I saw them, I could feel their pain, an echo of what I now carried. I understood why they sat in silence, why they released their minds; it was easier to forget, to become part of the living dead, than to hold the burden of what they'd seen and experienced.

◆◆◆◆

The wimple of the sister's habit was edged in sweat as she looked at the ledger in front of her.

"Lissie?" Her voice was thin, like a wisp of smoke. "Ah yes, she's here." She paused, blotting her forehead. "She was badly wounded when she arrived. Lost much blood." She looked up, saw my face registering a mixture of concern and alarm.

"Oh child, no need to worry now. I'll get the Mother Superior."

Moments later she returned with a large, imposing woman whose cheeks were amplified by the sharp cut of her habit. Around her neck, a weighty crucifix made of unpolished silver.

"You're here to see Lissie? You're her daughter?" She asked her questions quickly, as if she already knew the answers.

"Your mother is recovering well, but I will not let you excite her." The Mother Superior wrung her hands; I could tell she ran the hospital with efficiency and little patience for disorder.

"I will tell her you're here and come fetch you if she's well enough to receive visitors. Do you understand?"

I uttered a small, quiet "Yes." I realized I had been holding my breath, unable to interject as she spoke, worried that at any moment she was going to tell us that Mother was too ill, too fragile. But just as soon as she left, the Mother Superior returned, armed with the same stern look and strict instructions to keep Mother calm.

The door to her room was white, the paint peeling in small, soft curls. I was diligently focused on what was in front of me; I had concentrated to keep my emotions at bay, looking for small specks of dust or details in the woodwork as we walked. The door swung forward into a room with ten other beds. In the corner, propped up with pillows, my mother. Her face turned with anticipation toward the door. I can't recall if it was a sunny day, or if the room had windows, but her face glowed with a light that seemed to radiate from within her; I felt my throat constrict and heat flush beneath my cheeks.

"Mother—" I whispered. Anything else I had thought to say was caught in my throat, swollen with emotion. I sat in the chair arranged next to her bed.

"Oh, my dear Else," she whispered back, stroking my cheek. "The Mother Superior said that if I cried she'd make you leave, so," she patted my face lightly, "no tears."

"I'm so happy you're alive, Mama," I said, again resorting to my childhood name for her. In so many ways I felt like a young girl again; after weeks of managing our family, ensuring we had enough food, safe shelter, to be in the presence of my mother felt like a moment of peaceful surrender. She was still sick and unable to walk, but she was as she'd always been: my protector and refuge. I could, once again, release the responsibility I'd held onto tightly into her sweet provision.

She told me that she had lost even more blood after we left, that she was told her chances of survival were low. But that, here in Fridolfing, a Dr. Mueller was able to perform an operation that ultimately saved her life. She pointed to her leg, suspended above her bed in a delicate web of pulleys and cords.

"He set my hip and leg with pins," she explained. It would be months until she'd be able to walk, but eventually, she would without even the hint of a limp.

I stayed with her until the Mother Superior rushed us out. "Your mother needs her rest, child," she said, her face close to mine. Her words hurried as if they'd disappear before she could say them. Her breath smelled like onions.

Tony met me in the small makeshift lobby of the hospital. Peter and Joseph were outside, inspecting the collection of military vehicles that were parked in front of the building. I gave him a small smile. "Good," I said in English, nodding my head gently. His eyes lit up and, as if he couldn't help himself, he rushed forward, hugging me tightly.

"Good? Good!" His voice was raised with his normal American enthusiasm that I'd come to expect, but even then, this joy caught me off guard and I realized that I had been holding back any thread of hope out of fear that we'd experience the worst. But today confirmed what my heart had desired most fervently: my parents were alive. Both of them were alive. I had held my father's hand, had brushed my mother's hair. Had heard them speak for the first time since before the bombing.

Something in my body released and before I understood what was happening, I was sobbing. Tony, taken aback, tried to comfort me, mistaking my tears for sadness.

"Oh! Oh no, no, I'm sorry. Else? Oh dear." He was still patting my back trepidatiously when Peter and Joseph arrived, their brows furrowed. They joined Tony in his uneasy consoling.

All emotion drained, I fell asleep in the jeep as we drove back to Niedernfels, awaking only when we stopped outside the camp's main gate. As I smoothed back my hair and began to alight, Tony placed his hand on my arm, motioning for me to wait. He rummaged through a bag and pulled out three apples, two oranges, and a collection of small soaps.

"For you. And your sister. And brothers," he said in his broken Serbian. He smiled, then drew his face together, pursing out a small frown. "I'm...sorry." He waved his hands around his head sheepishly, as though he were taking responsibility for all of it—the bombing, my injured parents.

I shook my head and smiled back. "Thank you," I whispered, my eyes again filling with tears. I wanted to tell him how he helped me find hope again; that his offer to search for our parents, that seeing my mother and father had reignited a small ember of faith that our family would someday be reunited.

He had nothing to apologize for. None of us did. Me, Tony, Mary—in so many ways, we were still just children, forced to become adults before we were ready. I could hardly have imagined this life when I laid on the banks of Lake Bega with Anica and Sera. I thought of Tony dancing with his girlfriend at the camp's dining hall dances, how he dipped and swung her when the music went fast and wondered what he had dreamed up for his future before the war.

◆◆◆◆

Mother convinced her doctor to submit a request for a travel permit from the city hall, then asked the Polish man if perhaps he could help. Two months after the bombing, the boy, who brought his girlfriend meadow flowers, rode his motorcycle to Freilassing and told my father to get in. Wearing goggles and a helmet that was too small, he took to the road in a motorcycle's sidecar to be reunited with his wife. He'd tell his grandchildren that he squeezed into the sidecar like a turnip, but that nothing would stop him.

Chapter 21

Mary was breathless by the time she arrived at the door of our classroom-turned-apartment. It had been a week since I had seen our parents and the hopeful euphoria that I had brought back from my adventure with Tony was slowly starting to morph into an unsettled malaise. We knew where they were, but without a travel permit, we couldn't leave the camp to see them. And if we did secure one, Tony and Will had been assigned elsewhere. We didn't know any of the other American soldiers who visited on dance nights and had no one to ask for a ride to Fridolfing and Freilassing.

"Else!" she called from the threshold of the room. Her hands motioned quickly for me to join her, her eyes shining. I had been working on a letter to Mother that I had hoped to finish before setting out to get more food for Mary and the boys. I dreaded the long waits and was anxious to get a good place in the ration lines.

"What's going on, Mary?" I tried to soften the sharpness of my tone, to quell my obvious irritation at being interrupted. Mary giggled, unbothered, and grabbed my arm, pulling me down the hallway to the front door.

"Look!" She nearly shrieked as we walked into the courtyard. In front of us, a bicycle with faded green paint that was chipped on the handlebars. I looked at her incredulously and walked over to touch the seat, which was missing a few stitches.

"I thought we could—*you* could—use this to visit Mother!" She said as I slowly circled the bike, assessing its usability.

"Where did you find this, Mary?" I couldn't believe that she had somehow acquired this bike.

"Oh, it's okay," she said, brushing off my question. "We're only borrowing it." She grabbed the handlebars and walked it to me. "Try riding it!"

To figure out where Fridolfing was, where Mother was, in relation to the camp, I tried to remember the route Tony took when we returned after my first visit to her hospital. The roads were empty, but still well marked and I hoped that once I started I'd recognize landmarks well enough to find my way.

I rose early, before 6 am, and made sure the boys were taken care of for the day.

"Elseeeee, let me sleep," Frankie whined as I woke him.

"I need you to stay out of trouble today—and to help Mary get food, okay?" I tousled his hair.

"Yes, yes," he grumbled, rolling over. His almost immediate snores told me that there was only a small chance he had heard my instructions.

Mary packed a few slices of bread, a slice of cheese, and a small bit of meat into a satchel, which I placed in the basket attached to the front of the bicycle. As I wheeled it out of the gate, I looked down the long, expansive autobahn. It was empty and silent, except for a large crow cawing in the distance.

The ride itself wasn't difficult, the paved road nearly flat for the full 50 kilometers between the two cities. I took the Autobahn to the train station in Traunstein, made a left turn, then headed toward Fridolfing. By the time I arrived at the hospital, I had been pedaling for what felt like ages, but the sun had only crested into the sky so I knew it was still late morning. My feet, newly blistered and my legs, sore, I walked into the hospital to find Mother.

Our routine became well established—every other week I'd ride my bicycle the four hours it took to get the Fridolfing. Mother and I—and later, Father—would spend a few hours together, before I'd leave in the early afternoon in order to return before nightfall.

In June, Father had moved permanently from Freilassing to Fridolfing upon the recommendation of Dr. Mueller. Still unable to walk, my father was examined by the doctor, who recommended surgery that would ultimately result in a full recovery. In its immediate aftermath, the surgery rendered him immobile; his leg, like Mother's, set with pins, elevated above his head while he recovered in bed. His injuries were not as pronounced and while his recovery would be faster than hers, the first week I saw him in Fridolfing, his face was pale with pain.

"How are you feeling?" I asked as I pushed a lock of his hair across his forehead. He pressed his lips into a smile.

"Okay, Else. I'm okay." He looked toward the door. "I'm close to her, again," he said quietly, his voice straining with fatigue, but his eyes sparkling.

Chapter 22

"But Else, it's not fair that *you* get to see Mother and Father and that we have to stay here," Frankie muttered under his breath as he rolled his bedding into the corner of the classroom.

"Frankie." I pulled him in for a hug. At seven, he was still small enough for a cuddle. "Frankie, I'm afraid you're just too little. You're too small for the bike."

"But I could ride the handlebars." He squirmed away from me and slumped his shoulders.

"Hey! If Frankie gets to go with you to see them, then I get to go too," Joshi said from the other side of the room. By now he was twelve, but was tall enough to look a few years older.

"Joshi, of course." I sighed. "But we only have one bike. And I can't let you and Frankie go by yourselves."

I could tell they were disappointed. It had been months since they'd seen our parents. Mary missed them as well, but she was content to stay behind to help manage the family and had stayed busy working odd jobs around camp.

"Let me talk to Mary," I told them. "Maybe she can find us another bike to borrow and the three of us can go to Fridolfing next week."

Five days later, as the fog dissipated on the summer meadow, Mary waved us on our way as the three of us started down the Autobahn, in the direction of Traunstein. Joshi rode a girl's bike she had been able to procure (with her usual Mary magic), with Frankie riding on its handlebars.

Even though it seemed as if Joshi had grown at least a foot, and Frankie had sprouted up from the impish six-year-old that had ridden the open freight car only half a year earlier, they were once again her little boys as Mother held them in her arms and Father tousled their hair. Mother's eyes filled with tears as she stroked Frankie's hand while he sat on her bed, telling her about the different kinds of spiders and snakes he had found at the camp. I knew that she was thinking of Mathias and wondering if his blue eyes would have shone in the same way while looking for bugs; how Frankie would have been the perfect tutor to his younger brother.

We decided to spend the night and got permission to sleep in a small tent on the hospital grounds. We woke before dawn to the sounds of cows bellowing in the distance. Joshi had also rolled to the other side of the tent, taking all the blankets with him. Brushing the dirt off our clothing, we went inside to visit our parents. I saw the Mother Superior returning from the morning prayers in the chapel next to the hospital, wearing her silver crucifix, and quickly turned so she wouldn't see us.

We left when the midday church bells rang—Mother kissing both Joshi and Frankie so hard that they lost their balance.

The euphoria of seeing our parents gave us a burst of energy; we flew over the graveled road that led to Traunstein. When we reached the Autobahn, the smooth pavement proved too tempting for all three of us.

"I'll race you, Joshi," I said, feeling an unexpected swell of giddiness. I hadn't seen our parents that happy in months! Their smiles, our conversation—the entire visit felt like a step toward the comfort of sweet stability. We wouldn't have the bakery in Betschkerck, but perhaps we'd have a cozy home in the mountains of Germany, near an alpine lake surrounded by fir trees. I could almost taste the fragrance of the pine needles as we sped down the open road, Frankie shrieking with delight.

I paused my pedaling, coasting along the Autobahn, stacks of empty lanes on either side. Joshi was only a meter or so behind me and, closing my eyes, I realized how much I looked forward to these long bicycle rides through the German countryside as birds twittered their unending songs and the breeze hushed through the valley.

It was this moment of peace that made the metallic crash and howls of pain more pronounced. I pressed the brakes immediately, lurching forward as the tires skid against the pavement. As I turned around I saw the bike upended and Frankie looking down at Joshi who was writhing in pain, the bike on top of his body. I ran over. The skin from mid-calf to just above his knee had been peeled off, exposing an almost marbleized red and white scrape that filled with blood before it began to slide down his leg, onto the pavement.

"I think I'm okay." Joshi winced. Frankie and I pulled the bike off him, untangled his legs from the bar and helped him stand.

"Do you feel any pain?" I asked, feeling his arms and legs for breaks.

"Not, really, but—OW!" He had started walking and was now doubling over in pain. As the air made contact with his scrape, it began to sting; bending his knee only made it more pronounced as the wound stretched over his kneecap.

"Do you think you can still ride your bike?" I asked. We were only halfway to Niedernfels and still had 25 kilometers to go.

"I can try," he said, but nearly fell over in pain as soon as he began. "It's my knee. When I bend my knee, it hurts too badly."

I clenched my jaw and held my tongue. This was why I hadn't allowed them to go with me earlier, I thought. We were stranded in the middle of nowhere, with two bikes and one bleeding leg. I looked at Frankie. Perhaps he could ride the second bike and I could try to balance Joshi on my handlebars? But that thought was immediately dismissed as I watched Frankie hold up the bike with both hands, his head barely touching the bottom of the seat.

There was nothing else to do but walk. Joshi limped slowly alongside me while Frankie ran ahead, then waited for a few moments before running back to us. I held one bike in each hand, wheeling both next to me. When the wheels crossed over or the bikes wobbled into each other, we would stop to untangle the mess.

We had decided to walk through the woods instead of staying on the Autobahn hoping this would give us a more direct route back to Niedernfels. But as the sun started setting, I realized that nothing was going to help our journey move more quickly.

By dusk, my brow was covered in sweat, my hands sore from gripping the handles of both bikes so tightly in order to keep them upright. Joshi was silent; Frankie had stopped complaining, dragging his feet in exhaustion. As we navigated the uneven terrain, trying to circumvent roots that twisted the bicycles' wheels around, I tripped over a small branch that had fallen in a recent summer storm. I didn't fall, but instead crumpled slowly as I collided with the bikes' metallic frames. I turned over onto my back, feeling the damp dirt press into the back of my shirt.

I clenched my jaw. If I didn't, I would have screamed. "This," I said under my breath, "This is why I do this *alone.*"

The daylight was fading quickly. Both Frankie and Joshi were standing over me, looking concerned.

"Else, are you okay?" Joshi said quietly, as if he could sense that my frustration was moments away from bubbling over.

I looked up at the branches intertwining, the leaves glowing in the wake of the setting sun. "I'm fine," I replied, turning over, digging my knees into the dirt and lifting my body upright.

"I'm fine," I muttered, brushing off my pants, readjusting the bikes in my firm grip. This was the last time I'd bring the boys with me, I promised myself.

It took us another hour to reach the camp, the sun already set, the night dark and moonlit. Mary was clearly worried, her usual spark replaced with an almost anxious flicker that scooped up Frankie as soon as he walked through the door to our classroom apartment.

"I didn't know what to do when you weren't back by six," she said as Frankie tried to squirm out of her arms. I slumped to the floor, my back against the wall and fell asleep sitting up.

Chapter 23

By September, Father had been released from the hospital. As he eased his way out of the military vehicle that had driven him to the camp and we welcomed him back into our family rhythms, a gentle hum of gratitude seemed to surround us.

"Else! Look at all this food!" he marveled the first night as we sat down to a small feast celebrating his return. In the seven months we had been separated, Mary and I had become experts in the complexity of food permits, walking kilometers each day to pick up parcels of food from city hall. Frankie always helped me carry the bags when I walked through the camp's main gate, only occasionally sneaking a small tear of bread from the loaf.

In the coming months, our lives blurred with the mundanity of simple living, navigating the intricacies that seeped into our daily routines as a result of the bombing. Mother was still recovering from her injuries and subsequent surgeries so we applied for an apartment on the outskirts of Fridolfing to be closer to her hospital. On the crest of a hill, surrounded by farmland, I'd watch the fields turn from blue, to orange, to yellow as the sun rose while I walked into town each morning to do the daily shopping. Mary would walk with me on her way to the farm where she had gotten a job, helping a local family with household chores. When the hill sloped down into the town, she'd turn toward the large field that stretched westward and I continued on, basket and ration books in hand.

In March, Mother was discharged. Still fragile in her recovery, her homecoming was quiet, but I made sure to pick a bouquet of snowdrops that lined the dirt road that led to our apartment. They sat in a small glass vase on our kitchen table, greeting Mother as Father helped her through the threshold.

"Else," she breathed out, smiling. Her eyes were tired, but nothing could mask her happiness. I felt the well of gratitude overflow within my chest. She was here, alive. And as can only happen within the sweet serenity of a mother, a gentle blanket of comfort and safety enveloped us. She had survived. We had survived. That night I lay my head in her lap and fell asleep.

Mother had been discharged, but still needed rehabilitation treatments. Because her body was so frail, it was nearly impossible for her to walk up and down the hill from the apartment to the hospital. A stagecoach driver for the Weber Transportation Company would pick Mother up for her appointments, but otherwise, she rested in bed.

One morning I overheard Mother and Father talking in the kitchen.

"—if it's what we need to do, then I guess we'll have to do it," Father grumbled.

"I just think the doctor wants to make sure I'm able to get the treatment I need. And it's clearly too far from the hospital—"

"Are we moving again?" I said quietly, cutting Mother off.

She slowly lifted herself from her chair and began to make her way back to the bedroom.

"Only to be closer to town. Closer to the hospital." Her voice was still quiet, still weak. "The doctor is saying it's too difficult and expensive for us to be this far away. To have to rely on the stagecoach."

Our new lodging was a two-room apartment next to a farmhouse, filled with dust and old furniture. When we had arrived at Fridolfing's main square the day before, we soon realized no one would take us in. Mother sat on our bags, neatly stacked on the pavement, while Father walked toward city hall. Two hours later he emerged with a letter from the mayor.

"We're going down the road to a farm owned by—" he looked down at the letter, "Herr Mucke."

With some mayoral encouragement, the Mucke's took us in. The local government provided us with food, rent, and medical and general living expenses and we, again, eased into a new daily rhythm. Mother continued with her rehabilitation treatments while I took care of her and kept house. Mary did housekeeping for two families nearby. Father carried bricks all day for a local construction company and the boys went to grammar school.

In April 1946, Henry was discharged from the military and moved in with us, as well as our cousin, Nicola. The eight of us crowded into the apartment and made the most of the two rooms. Mattresses were pulled to the center of the floor every evening, then placed in closets once the day began. It was small, but we had spent so many years in equally small, crowded places that no one seemed to mind. We were finally together and that was all that mattered.

Henry got a job working at the Winkler farm taking care of the horses, leaving early in the morning and coming home by early afternoon. Soon he realized that Fridolfing and the surrounding towns hosted dances for the young adults living nearby and he'd hop on his bike most weekends to attend whichever dance was closest.

"I don't know how fun this sounds," I said one morning after Henry told us about every girl he danced with. "I'd rather play music than dance to it."

Henry laughed, pulling me up out of my chair and spinning me around the room. "But it's fun! See? Now you're a dancer!" I laughed and stumbled back to my seat, shaking my head. The military had pressed its thumbprint into Henry, but nothing could take away his impish smile and sense of fun.

"Besides," he continued, tearing off a piece of bread from breakfast," Mike and I always make sure the other one gets to dance with the prettiest girls." He smiled, the bread halfway out of his mouth.

"Mike?"

"I think you know him, Else." He started putting on his coat. "I work with him at the farm. He's a stagecoach driver. He said something about taking Mother to treatment last year. At the hospital. Surely you met him?" Henry brushed his hair forward, then back in three quick strokes. My brow furrowed as I tried to remember. Yes, there was a young man. Skinny, but kind; always very friendly. I tried to picture his face, but couldn't.

"I'm heading to town to check the mail." As he reached the door, he turned around. "Mike's stopping by so we can ride to the dance together. Come with us?" He swiveled his hips and mimicked spinning me on the dance floor. I smiled, and again, shook my head.

But that night, the door opened to his laugh, a bright, intoxicating thing. I saw his face and remembered and felt my stomach fill with flutter. As Mike stood at the door and said, "Hey Henry? Why don't we take Else with us?" I couldn't say no. I didn't think about how I couldn't dance, or how my shyness paralyzed any notion of following proper steps or the way I had dismissed the idea hours earlier. I only saw him smiling and said,

"Yes!"

Mike: Dachau 1943

The train stops. Or rather, doesn't simply stop, but screeches to a slow halt. The rumble of generalized talk ceased a few kilometers earlier, all of us tired and hungry and ready to be home after weeks of mud and bare bone exhaustion. Military training. When the metal of the train's wheels begin to grind against the metal of the train tracks, the silence that has settled among us amplifies its shriek.

"Why are we stopping," James whispers through clenched teeth, his inflection indicating more a statement of fact than question. We know that there is no room for expectation, no use trying to anticipate what will come next. During training, we were kicked, thrown down, made to run in the woods for hours on end until our heels bled. Breakfast was spoiled milk and stale bread. I was conscripted to fight a German war, but as a Polish-born Ukie, I know I am merely one body of many meant as the first line of defense on the front.

A German soldier steps into the train car, his uniform crisp enough to assume it has been freshly starched.

"What's he saying?" I whisper back to James.

"We have to get out," James says, already standing, already moving with the flow of bodies through the car's narrow door. We're herded into trucks, shoulder to shoulder, until no one else can fit. As we shove against each other, our teeth rattle and our limbs slap against the other men surrounding us, but still we keep quiet. It is as though we have taken an oath, assumed a vow of silence to preserve whatever lingering thoughts, ideas, and fleeting notions we still have. These are ours, not theirs, and so we pack them into our innermost sanctuaries and brace ourselves against the pockmarked road.

*The trucks stop outside a series of imposing brick buildings. We alight, falling into short lines while we wait for further instruction. We make a pitiful collection of conscripts, a lanky bunch made lankier still from the hard work and meager rations of training. We look forward, toward a gate of crisscrossed iron and move toward a small door in the middle with a phrase framed in iron: "*Arbeit Macht Frei.*"*

They stand us in a line and take any personal items, of which we had very few, then tell us to take off our clothes. We're marched into decontamination showers, our heads shaved before we're thrown into a new room where we pick through piles of clothes. I try to find trousers that stay up over my hips, a shirt with sleeves that aren't too long. At first, I try to find my old clothes, wondering if they had dumped out everything we had stripped off outside, but it only takes me a few moments to realize that it doesn't matter what I wear, only that I find something quickly as soldiers push and point and force us across the yard.

Surrounding the yard, which functions more like a town square, are drab buildings made of stone and brick. All ornamentation has been stripped away leaving austere boxes with the occasional window. As we push along, I barely notice the buildings, only my feet which now wear leather rat-chewed shoes. Later, I'll spend hours counting the bricks around the windows as we wait, standing in the square, at the end of each day.

We sleep in wooden bunks in long narrow barracks and wake before sunrise. My belly groans with hunger as we hurry outside, the cold early morning air cutting like a dull razor. Some men clump together for warmth, others stand in the two lines that have begun to form.

"Gehen!" *a soldier shouts pointing to the lines.* "Gehen!" *he bellows again, shoving me in their direction.*

I hesitate, not knowing where to stand. I see a woman with long hair plaited down her back. Even in the dark, I can tell her hair is red. She wears a long black skirt and holds a small child in her arms.

"Shhh, shhhh." She sways into the line furthest from me. I follow her. She walks in stilted steps, dropping her hand to her waist as she stops. I realize she had three other children near her, one clinging to her skirt, whimpering. I look down in front of me, bend my knees a little, and smile. "It'll be okay," I say in Polish. The child stops for a moment, her eyes meeting mine. "It'll be okay," I repeat, smiling, reaching down to squeeze her hand—

—I feel calfskin gloves on my collar as I'm ripped away. In the same moment, I hear the girl yelp, her whimper cascading into shrieks. My breath caught in my chest, I struggle to reorient myself.

"Diese Linie."

He throws me into a new line and we march forward into a day that becomes many days, but really just one long continuous day, up to our legs in mud, our hands calloused, our feet blistered. There isn't food, never really any food, just a piece of bread, or a potato with water. We dig trenches but we also dig out whatever humanity is left within us as the hours bleed into each other. Conversation means death. Eye contact means death. Weakness, death. Illness, death. Those that are too feeble, too strong, too frail, too forceful, too young, too old—the bodies pile around us, fester in our minds, make the air stink with rotted flesh.

Those of us who keep living, don't live.

Rabbis are paraded into the square and tortured.

There is the heat of summer. The oppressive cold of winter. The eager arrival of spring, her entrance heralded by rainstorms that fill in the trenches we dig until we're waist-deep in water.

As the sun grows hotter and I prepare myself for another year, we're shoved out of the barracks, back into the square. I watch the smoke uncurl from the chimney a few meters away.

"People," the man behind me spits, his voice hoarse. "That smoke—" he wheezed out "—people."

I watch the lines move across the square. Always, every day, lines to work, lines to barracks, lines toward the smoke, lines that never cross, but snake through the camp as if operated by an invisible hand. A hand that guides each column of people along their given track as if preordained.

I remember the scared eyes, the red braid, the girl wrapped in a long black skirt. Bile rises in my throat, mixing with the sour smell of ash that drifts down from the sky.

I wretch.

Chapter 24

I had grown up so fast, had fallen into a world of responsibility so early that I didn't know what it felt like to balance on the handlebars of a boy's bike as he rode through the dark with only a dim headlight; didn't know what it was like for a hand to reach toward mine, to hold it tight enough that I would forget where my own hand ended and his began.

Mike paid for my entrance to the dance, pulled me onto the dance floor, and in a whirl, I found myself on a new path toward a new life cocooned by the tender mist of young love.

The boy from school, who held my hand, who brought me wildflowers, whom I had promised to wait for, hadn't returned. Or rather, he never found me. But how could he? We had left Betschkerck for Hungary, then Austria, then what felt like dozens of little places—camps, towns, train stations—scattered throughout Germany. We were running, surviving, and, in many ways, moving further and further away from who we had been at the beginning of the war. Would I even recognize him had he arrived at our front door? Would he have recognized me? I could barely recognize the girl who lived in Betschkerck and helped her father with the bakery as she daydreamed about the sweetness of a teacher's life in her hometown.

I remembered the boy, how my heart raced as we embraced in the town square as the war marched toward us. A tender whisper of innocence in the midst of the unknown. But that heartbeat had changed, had been resculpted into a rhythm that reflected the fear and the trauma of loss. And because of that, or in spite of all we'd suffered, what pulsed through me now was richness that came with a life intent on living.

When I met Mike and, for the second time, my heart raced, it was different. Our youthful innocence gone, there was, instead, a recognition of something deeper than adolescent infatuation. And with this, we fell quickly, and madly, in love.

Three nights after the dance, I heard a knock at the door. As I cleaned our dinner dishes in the kitchen, laughter filled the front room and my heart leapt. Henry walked into the kitchen and leaned himself against the counter where the wash bin sat.

"Guess who's here, Else?" he said smiling. He grabbed the towel from my hand. "I'll finish this—you should go say hello to our guest."

I touched my hair in the mirror, smoothing the sides, and pinched my cheeks for extra rosiness. I couldn't help but smile as I walked into the room, mirroring his own as he passed his hat between his two hands nervously.

"Mike." I kept smiling. "It's so good to see you."

"It's good to see you too, Else," he said. "I thought I'd stop by to say hello to your mother. I haven't seen her since she was getting those treatments and I've heard that not only has she recovered, but she's walking again. I must see!" His eyes twinkled.

I laughed. "Ah yes, of course. I'll go fetch her," I said, knowing Mother could hear us in the next room.

He pulled me close and leaned into my ear: "A fair bit of warning, she may not be so eager to see me. Her roommate at the hospital was there because she had fallen off her bicycle while trying to avoid my stagecoach. But it wasn't my fault! I'd swerve to one side of the road—and she'd follow me. So I'd swerve to the other side of the road, and she'd follow me again. Until, with all the swerving, she toppled over. She tried to blame me, but she was just too clumsy to be on a bike to begin with!" He laughed out loud.

"Anyway, there's a chance she told your mother everything about this reckless stagecoach driver so I'll have to do a bit of convincing that I'm a nice, upright young man—" he paused and smiled "—worthy enough to come by to visit her daughter from time to time."

He sat with our family for hours that night. And the following night. Soon, Mike came over every evening after dinner. He'd beat my brothers in cards, tell us stories about his childhood in Poland. We knew that the war had separated him from his family, like it had with so many other families, and that he didn't know where they were or if they had survived, so we never pressed to hear about life before the war. But when he did talk about it, we saw beautiful lakes that stretched into long summer nights; dappled sunlight through forests filled with maple and ash trees. I'd close my eyes, remembering Bega Lake, how I'd run down the meadow with Anica and Sera after working the morning in the bakery.

Mike was jovial, always laughing, but when he talked of home, there was a softness that betrayed a quiet sadness that I knew he carried with him. We all did, in our own ways. It was hard to measure what had been lost, what we'd given up to simply survive. Mother's limp was another reminder, of sorts. How quickly we could have lost her, how miraculous her recovery; how beautiful this new gait. We held both grief and gratitude as we moved forward.

In summer, I worked for a local farm raking grass. Mike would borrow a motorcycle and come pick me up. I'd hop on behind him, holding his chest as he drove through town as fast as the bike would take us, my hair blowing in the wind.

One afternoon, we drove to the Salzach River. I watched Mike swim, still terrified from my near-drowning in Lake Bega to join him. As he dried off in the sun, we sat on the bank.

"Your German is good." I watched him towel off his hair, water dripping into his eyes. "Did you learn it in school growing up?"

"German? No." He shook his head quickly like a mutt, flinging water droplets into my face. I pushed him away, laughing.

"Mike!"

He laughed, rubbing the water out of his face with his open palm. "No, I only learned German after I was released from the work camp—when I started working as a stagecoach driver.

I remember one of my earliest trips, moving cows of all things across town, and I couldn't get the horses to slow down. They kept going faster and faster until they were at a full gallop. I kept calling to them to slow down, pulling the reins, but I lost control and the stagecoach went off the road, across a farm, and into a large window of the farmhouse."

As with most of Mike's stories, he dissolved into laughter as he told it. My eyes must have betrayed my shock.

"No, no, it was okay," he said, grasping my hands. "No one was hurt. Not even the cows. The *frau* was upset, but Weber Transportation Company fixed her window. What I realized, what my mistake was, was that I was trying to control the horses in Polish—and that they only understood German! So I made it my mission to learn German quickly so that me and the horses wouldn't surprise any more old German *hausfraus* in their front parlor."

I couldn't help but laugh with him. I imagined the old woman's face as she walked into her front room, finding horses, cows, and a very apologetic man who couldn't speak German. The stories she'd tell!

I also smiled because I, myself, was beginning to feel more and more like an old German *hausfrau*. Mother was doing well, but still needed help with taking care of our small but very crowded house. The days were full, but it felt like life had paused the moment the Germans marched into Betschkerck.

We had gotten used to living—surviving—day by day, but I wanted to be *alive*. I was only nineteen and I was ready to see what the world could be like now that the worst of it was over. Now that Henry was back. Now that Mother had survived. Now that we could begin to identify ourselves with something other than the war.

Chapter 25

Mike talked to Father in March 1948. We'd been in Fridolfing for nearly two years; I'd known Mike for the better part of a year. He didn't have a family, so our family became his, easily and quickly. His habit of coming over after dinner happened most evenings, and, depending on how the day went, we'd either tell stories or play games. Some nights we'd put on music and listen—or really, listen as best we could as Frankie and Joshi darted indoors from a game of pick-up football down the street or Mary told Mother stories from work that would have them both in stitches. The two-room apartment was small, but even with the constant frequency of activity, it was wonderful. We had almost lost everything, and yet here we were, together, Mike in the middle of all of it.

So when he talked to Father, it wasn't unexpected, but still felt like those evenings on his motorbike when he'd speed through the fields, my arms wrapped tightly around his waist, my hair blowing in the wind. It was a total thrill.

Father called me into the kitchen where they were talking. I had been waiting with Mother, Mary, Henry, Joshi, and Frankie, in the other room. We all sat in the silence, eyes darting from one to another, each trying not to giggle. I fiddled with my handkerchief, the one with lace trim and an embroidered E. I traced my finger along the lines of the letter until I heard Father call my name, dropping the handkerchief onto the floor.

He asked me (his eyes sparkling) if I wanted to marry Mike.

I remembered the moment we crossed the bridge over Lake Bega, my teeth slamming together as my body shook from the explosion of sulfur and stone; the open train car; Mathias's blue eyes; the blood running down Mother's leg; the twisted metal of the bombed-out train station.

I thought of summer nights, of riding on handlebars, and swinging to dancehall tunes; lazing afternoons on the river and idling conversations that eased out of us, like honey—sweet and slow.

The memories rushed in at the same time: the darkest nestled within the brightest moments of the last five years. How could I have one without the other? For only an instant, sadness washed over me with the realization that without the sorrow, I wouldn't feel this deep happiness; that each step away from Betschkerck, away from Yugoslavia, had brought me here to this moment.

I smiled, my eyes crinkling. "I never thought I'd get to marry a Ukrainian."

Mike erupted in laughter and pulled me into his arms.

◆◆◆◆

Saturday morning, April 24, we got married. The sky was a pale blue, delicate like a piece of silk had been pulled across the horizon. Mother had found a beautiful dress: long sleeves with a smart collar and a dainty train. I wore silk gloves and kitten heels, with a headpiece that had been customized just for me. Made of flowers and organza, the band had arcs of baby's breath and gardenias and sat on the crown of my head with a veil that fell down my back.

I arrived with Mary, my maid of honor, to the town square. Mike was waiting for me, with Henry, his best man. We went into the town hall, where the mayor, who had helped my father find us work and the apartment, presided over our legal marriage ceremony. Mike squeezed my hands as he pronounced us husband and wife. I couldn't stop smiling.

When the doors opened back onto the town square, it was as if the entire village had arrived to escort us to Mariä Himmelfahrt for the sacrament of marriage. Someone hollered—and then another. And then another! Until the crowd erupted in cheers as we walked through the path of people that had parted in front of us. In the distance, I heard bells and for a moment, they were from John of Nepomuk in Tschetereg. I was once again small, with braids that fell over my shoulders, taking delight in the pine trees that fell along the cascading hillside. I had always thought I'd stay where I was born, that I'd marry the boy from school, and that we'd join the generations of family that had planted roots, ours entwined with those who had come before us. And that it would continue into the future, generations upon generations linked to the land, to this place into perpetuity.

But as the bells brought me back to Fridolfing, to Mike, to this man from a different place, with severed roots, I felt more than just bridal effervescent bliss, but deep happiness. Our union would begin the tender buds of new growth. We were both so far from what had been our homes, both strangers in a strange land. But we had each other and it was more than I could have ever imagined.

Shortly after we were married, I found out we were expecting our first child.

Chapter 26

Our first weeks and months of newlywed contentment was filled with nervous delight. We secured an apartment on the first floor of the building where my family lived. It was a small apartment, but furnished with a bed, table, four chairs, and a wood-burning stove. Mike was no longer a stagecoach driver, so he spent most days of the week traveling to neighboring villages, looking for work. Now that the war was over, work for non-Germans was suspended as jobs were re-prioritized for German soldiers returning from the front and their families.

"I'll find something, Else." Mike touched my shoulder as we sat at our little table, late spring's dusk filling the room with blooms of blush and orange. "We have the unemployment aid," he continued. Only 75 Reichsmarks a week, I thought to myself. "Plus, I have my savings from when I worked at the stagecoach company. That's nearly 10,000 Reichsmarks. That will help us make ends meet while I keep looking and allow us to prepare for the baby."

He smiled and placed his hand on my stomach.

"Do you think it's a boy or a girl?" I knew he was changing the subject, but I didn't mind. I had become increasingly worried about how we'd be able to take care of ourselves, of our family. For so long the future didn't matter—we only needed to get to the next town, the next job, the next day—and now it was all I could think about.

"Whatever this baby is," I responded, cupping my hand over his, "he or she will be perfect."

"And we'll be able to give them the perfect home," he added, kissing me on the cheek.

The next week, I left the apartment to get that week's ration cards. By now, ration books and cards and coupons had become so normal that I could barely remember a time when we didn't have to use them. I had decided that week I'd see if I could get a little extra sugar—perhaps from Mary and Mother—to make a small cake for Mike. My wifely duties compelled me to lift his spirits during his frustrating, seemingly unending, job search.

It was newly summer and the humidity threatened to linger in the air. I knew that as we approached July, and then August, that it would only become more unbearable and I wondered how I'd manage with a growing belly. I was thinking these thoughts, absentmindedly touching my stomach, when I found myself at the front of the line.

I nearly missed hearing the woman in front of me stutter to the office manager, "But, sir, what—what does this mean?"

"Next!" he said sternly, motioning me to step forward. In my hand he placed a series of bills.

"No." I shook my head. "I'm here for the ration cards."

"Today you're getting the new Deutschemarks instead." He began counting out the next set of bills. "You have forty there, you'll get twenty more later." His eyes were fixed on his hands as they sorted the paper money in front of him. "You'll be able to exchange your Reichsmarks and Rentenmarks for a limited time. Next!" He waved his hand, motioning me to move to the side for the next person in line.

I looked for the woman who was in front of me, who seemed just as confused as I was, but she had already left. As I walked home, I saw hurried, whispered conversations and frantic gestures. Was there really a new currency? That had arrived to replace the old one overnight?

Hours later, Mike shuffled through the front door, his feet moving slower than normal. As he walked into the kitchen, I placed the money on the table.

"We have Deutschemarks now," I said grimly.

"I heard," he said. "That's all anyone could talk about today." He ran his hands through his hair. I knew he was thinking about the Reichsmarks he had saved. "I'll see if I can exchange everything tomorrow."

In the morning, he left with 10,000 Reichsmarks and came home with 60 Deutschemarks.

◆◆◆◆

"What will we do?" I whispered. It was dark, hours after the sun had set. I couldn't muster the courage to ask when Mike showed me the money, all of which could fit in the palm of one hand. I busied myself with cleaning the house, making dinner, but couldn't bring myself to speak.

Only after we climbed into bed and Mike's arms found their familiar spot around my waist did I allow myself to feel the fear that had crept behind me all day. I felt my voice catch in my throat. Mike didn't answer, only stroked my hair.

Hours later, still awake, still silent, I moved my head to look out the window. I saw the moon, nearly full, its light peeking through the curtain. We had come this far, survived this much. Is this how it would end? I knew, without turning, that Mike was also still awake. My hand searched for his and, as our fingers interlaced together, I promised myself that we'd find a way to survive this too.

◆◆◆◆

Mike got up before the sun rose. His side of the bed was still warm when I awoke, the morning light trickling into the apartment; he hadn't been gone long. I knew enough not to worry, but I couldn't help but feel a kind of unfamiliar unease. We hadn't reached the point of desperation, but a hopeless shadow had begun to fall on this temporal, idyllic newlywed dream and I wasn't sure what would happen. I knew we were fighters—both of us. But we could only fight when there was something to fight *with.* No money and no job left us with so little, but I knew I'd find the scraps that would allow us to scrape by.

By the time he came home, the sun was beginning to set on the long summer day. It was late and my insides churned with worry until I heard his key in the door, its latches heaving forward. Mike walked in with a proud smirk, a bag slung over his shoulder. Without saying anything, he emptied its contents on the table: Three small onions, a head of lettuce, and a few potatoes, still covered in dirt.

"Where—" I stuttered with surprise. "Where did you get all this?"

"I asked!" he replied. "Well…not so much as asked, but explain to some of the farmers that my wife was pregnant, that I couldn't get a job on account of being Ukrainian, and that any money we had—" He made a flicking motion with his hand.

"I don't think we're the only ones, Else" he said, looking at my face which had taken on a mixture of surprise and bewilderment. "I think a lot of people are hard up for food and need a little help."

"But…begging?"

"Not begging. Asking to see if there's anything to spare. The smallest onions. The greenest potatoes. We can make do on whatever people are willing to give."

I learned how to make soup with water, potato, and leeks; bread from old grain. I was always hungry, an unfortunate and ill-timed symptom of my pregnancy, but was able to satisfy any craving without mentioning it to Mike.

In early September, I woke up with the taste of salt on my tongue and an incredible desire for bacon. I pushed away the thought, knowing we couldn't afford meat and that even the most generous farmer wouldn't give up anything from their smokehouses.

I sat at the table and closed my eyes. It was almost fall and the light had shifted into its golden harvest hue. I hadn't eaten much meat since we lost our money; my body felt weak and anemic. And I couldn't stop thinking about bacon.

"Else?" Mike walked over to where I sat, bending his knee so that his face looked at mine. "Else, are you okay?" He brushed hair away from my face. "You look pale."

My eyes met his. "I can't tell you," I said, my eyes beginning to well up. I tried to make it stop, pushed away the tears before Mike could see them, but it was no use. I started sobbing, my head in my hands.

"Else!" Mike's voice rose with concern. "Please! Please tell me what's wrong." He wrapped his arms around me. "Please Else. You're scaring me."

I sniffled, looking up at him. "I just…" I started crying again. "I just really want some bacon."

Mike pulled me in tighter. I felt his body shake as he tried not to laugh.

"My dearest wife, if you need bacon, I will get you bacon." And with that, he walked out the door.

When he returned with a skinny slab of bacon wrapped in waxed paper, I couldn't believe it. When I asked how he managed it, he shrugged his shoulders and said, as he lit the stove, "Nothing you need to worry about."

Years later, Mike would tell me how he ran down the road to a farm where he had seen pigs out to pasture. He knocked on the door, and was surprised when a woman answered, wearing overalls and a kerchief.

"Hello *Frau,*" he said, taking off his hat. "I'd like to speak to the owner of the farm."

"That's me," she replied.

Still surprised, he began to make his case—but, still flustered and hellbent on finding bacon, his usually slow, methodical petition became a rushed, urgent plea.

"You told her what?!"

"I told her that my pregnant wife desperately needed bacon and that if she couldn't get me any..." He smiled sheepishly "... that I'd just go get it myself. And pointed to one of the pigs."

I still think about the bacon—it was the best I ever had. We fried it up that night and I ate every single piece. My head swirled with delight as I went to bed.

But the bacon wasn't enough to sustain us for more than a day. And while the farmers were generous when they could be, we struggled to make ends meet. Mike sold his Bulova watch, which buoyed us through the next month or two. Soon that money ran out and we were left, again, with nothing.

As the snow began to fall, and the glow of Christmas enveloped the town, we sat near the stove in our apartment, trying to keep warm.

"Else, we can't keep living like this," Mike said, finally breaking the silence that had sat with us since dinner.

"I know," I replied quietly. I ran my fingers across my swollen belly. The baby would be here soon and we were only able to ration one or two sticks of firewood a night.

"I've been looking into what it would take to go to America," Mike began. I quickly lifted my head to look at him.

"There's an organization called the Polish Organization for the Resettlement of Displaced Persons. They're based out of Chicago and might be a way for us to really start our life together." He dug a piece of soot out of his nail bed. "I don't know what else we could do here, Else. I don't know how long it'll take for jobs to open up to non-Germans." He dropped his head and said, nearly in a whisper. "And we can't go back to Poland."

"Or Betschkerck," I replied, quietly.

This was the truth we knew we had to confront, eventually. That this wasn't our home—had never been our home, even though it was where we finally found happiness after so many years of sorrow. Yes, my family was here, but Mike was my family. This baby was my family. And we needed to find a way to do more than merely survive. We owed it to ourselves to try to make a life worth really living.

Chapter 27

It took weeks to gather all the required documents: identity records, birth certificates, certification of residence, emigration permits, work certificates, confirmation of employment, letters from my Uncle Joe, our American sponsor, and a screening with a selection committee to determine if we were eligible to immigrate to the United States. All the while, as we collected and filled out forms as we talked to officials and stood in long lines, I felt my bones shift as I walked, my stomach growing larger still.

The year had clicked to 1949. Eight years since the Nazis had invaded Yugoslavia; nearly a lifetime away from our home in Betschkerck. I knew that the baby was going to come any day, and while we waited to hear back from the resettlement organization, we also waited for our baby to arrive.

Two weeks into the new year, as a storm moved across distant mountains toward Fridolfing, I felt my stomach contract, a sharp ache shooting through my back. It might be nothing, I told myself, cradling my stomach as I walked. It happened again, only minutes later, the contraction causing me to fall into the chair. I waited for the pain to pass. I called out to Mike.

We made quick work, packing a bag before walking upstairs to my parents' apartment. It was nearly midnight and the storm had settled onto the fields, raging outside the windows while we walked slowly toward their apartment door. My mother came into the hallway before we could knock.

"I'm sending the boys downstairs," she said as Frankie and Joshi dashed around her.

"I get the bed!" I heard Joshi shouting to Frankie, who responded with, "Not if I get to it first!" And a cascade of laughter.

The storm rattled the windows as I lowered myself into the bed. Mary had run to get the midwife and as the lightning flashed, I remembered the warm morning of Mathias's birth, running through town, pleading with the midwife.

"I hope she doesn't have to finish morning prayers," I gasped through another contraction, closing my eyes as my body squeezed against the pain.

The lights went out. Only lightning. Then the soft glow of candlelight, multiplying as Mother set each newly lit taper on near the bed. There was the crack of thunder, then quiet, then pain. Light, dark, stillness, shrieking—the cadence flowed around us, within us, as though propelled by a current of living rushing toward new life.

Mike held a candle that wavered with his nerves and I counted the flickers on his face as the contractions increased in intensity.

Michael was born just before dawn on January 17th. Nine pounds, with sweet blue eyes that reminded me of Mathias. He opened his small mouth to scream.

I looked at Mike as Michael nestled into my breast, a tuft of soft downy hair against my skin. And I? Nothing. Only silence and the sweetness of unspeakable joy.

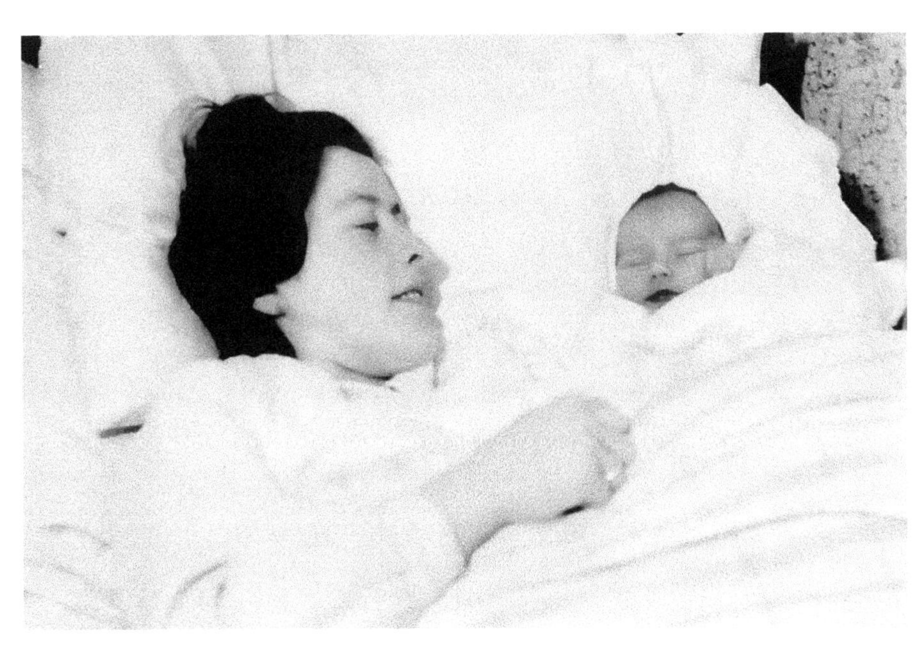

EPILOGUE

In June of 1950, we received a letter that our documents were accepted and that we would be admitted to the United States as displaced persons. That fall we took a train to Munich, then another to Bremerhaven in Northern Germany, on the North Sea. A former German military base, it was now occupied by American soldiers who ran it as one of the largest forced displacement camps, housing as many as 5,000 emigrants waiting to begin their journey to a new home. Every day I walked with Micky to the camp office to check the departure board for our names. A few weeks in, we saw them, scratched in chalk.

After the medical exams, we took another train to the ship's dock and, on December 12, 1950, we boarded *USNS General R.M. Blatchford.* On December 22, we pulled into New York Harbor. As the Statue of Liberty came into view, I couldn't believe we had truly made it. Uncle Joe had sent $13 through the Polish Organization for the Resettlement of Displaced Persons, which was handed to us by one of their representatives as we walked off the ship. The organization also paid for our transportation to Chicago by train, which we would repay, as a one-time fee, after we'd been U.S. residents for one year. The station was crowded, the noise so different from the creaking ship hull, the quiet streets of Fridolfing. As the train pulled out of the station, I took Micky to the observation car.

"Look," I said, as I hoisted him up, pressing my finger gently into his soft belly. "We've arrived, my sweet baby." I kissed his cheeks. "Look at where we are!"

The woman standing next to us tapped me gently on the shoulder. In her hands, a large Hershey chocolate bar. She motioned for me to take it, and then again when I tried to refuse. It had been so long since we'd had chocolate—long enough that I couldn't remember if Micky had ever tried anything so sweet. I placed a small square in his hands. His fingers wrapped around the candy, and he smiled his toothy toddler smile.

I saw the bar begin to melt, and then, in one rushed motion, his little hand shoved fully into his mouth. Chocolate was everywhere, and of course it was. I had forgotten that it melted in your hand if you waited too long. I had forgotten the way the sugar made everything a little sticky. I licked my fingers and tried to wipe the chocolate off his cheeks, tasting the sweetness that now spread all over his face. He loved it, all of it—the chocolate bar, this game we had instantly created of Micky dodging mama in fits of giggles. It reminded me of watching Father knead dough at the bakery in Betschkerck; Anica and Sera picking me up on our way to school; Mother glowing as her stomach swelled with Mathias.

My childhood had ended so quickly, had been ripped from me as the war enveloped our lives. When Mike and I boarded the train for Munich, leaving Fridolfing behind, my heart ached for one last dinner in our small kitchen in Betschkerck, the smell of the bakery ovens wafting into the room while Mother busied herself with dinner and Father threw Frankie over his shoulders. On the boat, my stomach lurched as the waves buoyed us further away from everything that was familiar, crest by crest. But as we sat on the train that sped toward our new home and Micky shrieked with happiness, I realized that what we had left behind—a tapestry of joy and sorrow—was for this… The simple delight of a precious life worth living.

Acknowledgments/Ritt

I want to thank my brother Micky who provided a constant source of support and authentication for Else's Journey. From the bottom of my heart, I thank my collaborator Kelley who is a brilliant writer and inspirational storyteller. This book would not have been written without her.

It is with deep gratitude that I acknowledge Paul, my dear friend of over 30 years who served as an ongoing mentor, expert in WWII history, and reader of manuscript drafts. He was instrumental in the initial concept of the source materials that served as the foundation for the book.

I thank my husband Rick and children Andrew, Heidi, and Paul who shared their recollections of stories told to them by Else and encouraged me to continue this journey. I am incredibly grateful to my extended family, friends, and colleagues who took the time to provide feedback and check in to see how things were going. They gave me the courage to continue even when overwhelmed.

My greatest appreciation is for my mother Else who graciously shared her story as a young woman living an unexpected life during WWII.

Acknowledgments/Hartman

Else came into my life when the former chair of Columbia College's English and Creative Writing department, Pegeen Reichart-Powell, forwarded an email to my MFA cohort from Elizabeth, asking for help to tell her mother's story. I am deeply grateful for the spark that inspired me to reply and brought me into this beautiful experience. My gratitude to Elizabeth for trusting me with the details of Else's life. My many thanks to teachers and peers at Columbia College who read early drafts of the manuscript. When I started this project, I had just found out I was pregnant with my first child. As I write these words, I'm due with my second. Experiencing motherhood has made this work more meaningful and has further illuminated the vulnerability of women, children, and families in times of war. To lead someone deeper into empathy is a profound gift, and I thank my children for all the ways that they've done this. And of course, to my heartbeat, Jesse - how could I tell any story without you by my side?

About the Author/Ritt

Elizabeth Ritt was born and raised in Chicago, IL, and is the proud and loving daughter of Mike and Else. She enjoys reading historical fiction, memoirs, and mystery novels. Elizabeth is a professor of nursing and loves to teach but most of all learn from her students.

About the Author/Hartman

Kelley Hartman lives in Chicago with her husband and two children. She has her MFA in creative nonfiction from Columbia College Chicago.

www.ingramcontent.com/pod-product-compliance
Lightning Source LLC
Chambersburg PA
CBHW041752010726
47507CB00009B/367

9781955791939